the Home Crowd

After ten years in Australia, George Fielden
abandons friends, career and bride-to-be to return
to the north of England, and to those he left
behind. From his uncle's derelict farm in West
Yorkshire and from the wilds of the moors, he
seeks out traces of the life he never lived, stalking
another past and another future in the form of his
old girlfriend Kate.

When contact comes however, it shakes all hope
of easy reconciliation and offers up stark choices
instead. Emotionally and physically displaced,
George is torn between Australia and England,
and who to leave behind. And overshadowing his
decisions is the omnipresent menace of Kate's
boyfriend, Vic.

*The Home Crowd* is an absorbing, compelling story
about the power of the past and the importance of
belonging.

*Cover photograph: Fay Godwin, Crow Hill, above Mytholmroyd.*

Graham Kershaw was born in 1961 in Rochdale, Lancashire, and emigrated with his family in 1971 to Western Australia. He graduated from the University of Western Australia with Honours degrees in English (1984) and Architecture (1993). He currently practices as an architect in Fremantle, where he lives with his wife and daughter.

*The Home Crowd* is his first novel. He has previously published short fiction in Australian literary journals.

# the Home Crowd

### GRAHAM KERSHAW

**FREMANTLE ARTS CENTRE PRESS**

First published 2002 by
FREMANTLE ARTS CENTRE PRESS
25 Quarry Street, Fremantle
(PO Box 158, North Fremantle 6159)
Western Australia.
www.facp.iinet.net.au

Consultant Editor Wendy Jenkins.
Production Coordinator Cate Sutherland.
Cover Designer Marion Duke.
Typeset by Fremantle Arts Centre Press
and printed by Griffin Press.

National Library of Australia
Cataloguing-in-publication data

   Kershaw, Graham, 1961- .
   The home crowd.

   ISBN 1 86368 370 4.

   I. Title.

   A823.4

The State of Western Australia has made an investment in this project through ArtsWA in association with the Lotteries Commission.

Publication of this title was assisted by the Commonwealth Government through the Australia Council, its arts funding and advisory body.

*For my parents,*
*Norman and Ruth Kershaw,*
*who did a good thing.*

# FIRST HALF

*Glory often coincides with the birth of superficial relationships.*

Eric Cantona

# I

Forty minutes north of Manchester airport it seemed like the whole of England was one long stream of grey terraced houses, boarded-up shops and off-licences. They rolled past the bus window like a depressing home movie, one that might never end, until the long stone facade began to stutter and gather little punctuations of green. Shops and signs grew rare. I saw grass, then fields.

Through the misted windows a wash of murky green descended like rain over a deepening valley. Frozen stiff at the back of the bus, I watched the overweight women and the wheezing men sway and I tried to imagine their thoughts. I couldn't even start. After ten long years away they all seemed very foreign to me, with their shapeless arctic jackets and their blanched skin.

I got off at what I prayed was the right stop and watched the bus disappear around the bend. The last exhaust vapours were swept away by savage little gusts of wind, then it was just me. In either direction the road snaked away along the floor of the valley and was swallowed by thick mist. The bare frames of trees on either side held up a low ceiling of cloud.

It was miles north of the area I knew well, and the light was fading. Tramping past a railway viaduct, case in hand, I took the first turn right across the canal bridge, following my A to Z and distrusting Stan's directions. Not for the first time I thought of sunny, sandy Fremantle and of Vanessa in one of those new beachside cafes, looking utterly self-satisfied.

The road ahead curved sharply into the mist, straight up along the high side of a deeply wooded combe. At least I assumed it was a 'combe'. That was one of those words I picked up at university in Australia. It wouldn't have been a 'combe' if I'd stayed around in England and become a dustman — it would have just been a Bloody Horrible Place To Be On A Wet February Evening.

The black net of branches sank away out of sight below as I stumped up the slippery road, shifting the case from one hand to the other to ease the strain. At the top was a T-junction, and it seemed lighter coming out of the woods, but night obviously wasn't far away. Lights were already shining from new houses across the road: squat pebbledash jobs with huge garages. They all looked lost, those little houses, up there on their own.

To the left, my map book said the track narrowed before reaching Stan's door, but my eyes were drawn straight ahead and upward, where the clouds had parted to expose a naked hillside studded with dark stone amongst the grass and gorse. Crowning it, like a steel spike driven into its skull, was an enormous stone obelisk with a pyramid cap, black against the sky. As I paused there, cloud swept down from the west and swallowed the monument whole. Rain drifted in.

Beyond the new houses, the road eventually petered out to a dirt track. Below it, facing the invisible valley, three dark stone buildings formed a yard. The largest showed light at its lower windows. As I got closer, I recognised Stan under its porch, stooped as if the little roof were too low. He had dirty blue overalls on, open to the waist.

'Find it all right, then?' he called, as I dragged my wet case to a halt over the gravel. He had his hands on his hips and he took up the whole porch. 'How's y' father?'

I stood out in the rain with water running down my face and looked for signs of humour. All I saw was how he'd dried up over the years, into a shrunken, creased version of the Stan of old. 'He's dead, Stan. Dad died last month. You know that.'

'All right, all right. Don't get all shirty. Wasn't sure you'd know, that's all. Never saw hide nor hair of you, did he?'

Water ran down my back. 'Do you think I could come in, Stan? Only it's a bit —'

'Uncle Stan to you.'

'I feel stupid saying that at my age.'

'Aye, well you'll feel stupid suckin' y' dinner out through a straw too, if y' call me owt else. At your age.' Leaning out for effect, he squinted upward and seemed to notice the rain for the first time. 'Come on,' he said and closed his own door behind him with a bang. 'I'll see you to the shed.'

On the far side of the yard stood something like a cottage, but far too small. It was more like a box than a building — a black stone box, glistening in the rain, every edge of every tight-fitting block as sharp as the day it was cut. Even the roof was stone: fat slabs of slate, lapped tight, ridge to eave. There was only one visible opening — an arched doorway just off-centre, with a timber door set inside, painted white.

I thought of a lighthouse, or a keep. 'But it's beautiful, Stan.'

Stan was fumbling with keys. 'Eh?' From below dripping eyebrows he looked at me now as if I'd said it was a turd.

'I like it. Did you build it?'

'Oh, aye. I built it. Just before the bloody Roman Empire, that was. Did I ever, y' daft bugger. The bloody thing must be two hundred year old.' He was still struggling with the keys, squinting at them in the dark. His hands looked red and shaky, and veins stood out on the back. 'The hot water system I did do, but that's only a hundred.'

'Who's was it then, originally? Weavers?'

'Halifax Building Society, as far as I know.' The door swung in and Stan turned his heavy, thatched eyes on me. 'Don't go losing that,' he said and slapped the long cold key onto my wet palm, 'because I've no other.' He spun away on the gravel then and was gone.

Inside I found a table and two chairs against one wall

and a sideboard that doubled as a kitchen bench against the other, next to an old fireplace with a gas stove set inside. Over an alcove created by the tiny bathroom, steep timber steps led up to a shelf. Hopefully with a big fat bed on it.

The walls were stone like the outside, but unblackened and dry. I had to look back, to check the door was really closed, it felt so cold. There was a kettle under the sink, so I tried to light the stove, but the matches were damp. My hands wouldn't move properly: they had ugly red welts across them from holding the case. Stamping my feet, I shook my jacket off and on a second attempt got the kettle going.

I sat in the corner chair with a steaming cup in my hands for a long time, trying to calculate times across the world. I woke some time later to find an empty cup in my hands. A bare light bulb hummed overhead. It was still dark at the window. I climbed the stair with the walls oscillating around me and fell on the bed. The pillow was hard, but the darkness was soft, so I let myself nestle into it, pulling the stone-grey blankets over my head.

I woke the next day into the dimness of a late afternoon. In my thickest jumper and an extra pair of socks, I lit the oven and cantilevered what body parts I could over its open door. Then I set the kettle going and looked in the sideboard. This was my best moment yet, because Stan had put bread and jam in there.

By sitting on the table rather than in the chair, I could eat my jam butty and look out on the fields below, picked out in wavering lines by broken drystone walls. Stan was out there, about fifty yards downhill, staggering stiffly across the nearest field between two stone huts. Back trouble, I thought, and maybe a hangover. No wonder he's turned into such a grumpy bastard. Still, he looked the part: the rugged northern farmer, hard as the wind, a craggy-faced beast with the heart of a lamb.

Except I knew he was no more a farmer than me. He'd been a lot of things before inheriting the farm five years ago — a builder, a debt-collector, then a debt-dodger. He'd even been a security guard for a few years, but not a farmer. What did him in, Dad used to reckon, was losing Joyce straight after getting the farm. 'But then,' Dad would say with his usual humanity, 'Stan always was a boozer.'

I watched now as Stan stooped to lift something out of the grass. He had to straighten up quick-smart, holding his back. 'You've got your hands full here,' I said out loud. 'I'd leave you to it, but I need the use of your car.'

I crunched over the yard an hour later and rapped the knocker hard against Stan's door. He only poked his head out at first, then he let the door fall open a little more and took a good look at me. I instantly regretted the Calvin Klein jumper that Vanessa had insisted on.

'Did y' find the loaf?' he demanded.

'Oh, hi. Yes, er, Uncle. Delicious, thanks.'

'I suppose you'll be needing more than that, if y' staying. You are staying?'

'Yes. If that's okay. I was wondering about buying myself some stuff in town.'

'I drive Wednesdays.'

'Right. Only it's Thursday, isn't it? Today, I mean.'

'Aye.'

'So-o ... maybe I could borrow the car?'

'Or maybe you couldn't. Joyce never lent the car out in her life. It's not mine to lend, is it? It's Joyce's.'

There seemed no answer to this. He expected me to go, I could tell, but I just stood there. I needed his phone at least, if I couldn't get the car. 'It's all right, then, if I stay for a few days?'

'No skin off my nose,' he said, aghast, and looked down the road as if expecting more guests. Then we stared at each other again. 'Well, you'd best come in,' he said at last, with great resignation. 'I'm just about to make some tea. You'd best join me.'

Words of thanks died on my lips as I picked my way through the car parts and clothes on the floor of the hall. Beyond was the sort of living room that might have been cosy if it hadn't been totally disgusting. There was a tall bank of narrow windows on the far wall, divided by deep stone mullions. Miraculously, they showed slices of sunshine moving over the green hills across the valley. There was a clock on the mantelpiece, but it had stopped — probably when Joyce stopped winding it — and it was swamped now by unopened mail.

'Sit yourself down then,' Stan ordered over his shoulder, as he disappeared into the adjoining kitchen. 'I just have to see to the sheep, then I'll be back onto tea.'

There was nowhere to sit without moving newspapers and oily rags, so I looked for the phone instead. I counted six framed photos along the way: Joyce marooned in a soft sofa; Joyce with my mum and her sister Alice, in the best floral polyester that 1976 could buy; a younger Joyce squinting into the sun before an icy lake; Joyce (twice) with half a pint, in the pub (same booth, different frocks); and central on the mantelpiece, free of clutter, a sharp black and white Joyce as bride. On top of the television was another I could only glance at, it reminded me of Mum so much — a shrunken Joyce in bed in a pink nightie, her face washed-out by the flashlight.

I found an old black phone and directory on the sideboard in the hall, under the Manchester Evening News. With an ear out for Stan, I hurriedly looked up the name I was after and rang the number. It was in Soppstone, which was quite close if I remembered right, and it was ringing at my ear as the back door banged. That made me panic and I dropped the heavy handpiece down with a crash.

Stan was standing in the doorway to the kitchen picking mud off a boot onto the carpet. He was watching me calmly. 'If you've any use for the phone, you only have to say.'

'Yes. Right. I'll give you something for it. I was just trying Vanessa.'

'It must be four in the morning over there. Early riser is she, your betrothed?'

'Yes.'

'Must be. Did y' get the international tone, then? Joyce couldn't get it on that thing. She always used to use the one in here.'

'Right. What's for tea, then?' I rubbed my hands together and looked kitchen-ward.

He was still looking at me. 'Well, I had a can of beans and another of spaghetti, so I thought I'd save the gas.' He waited, challenging me to stay.

'Wouldn't have any veggies about, would you? You know — Fresh Country Fare, all that?'

'No, I bloody well wouldn't. Unless you eat grass.' He turned back to the kitchen then, mumbling, 'What do you think this is, a bloody cafe?' He emptied tins into a pan while I watched, then lit the gas. 'You'll like it or lump it.' he added, then turned and caught me with sharp grey eyes. 'I told you how I was fixed when you rang. No one asked you to come.'

'No, they didn't.' I held his glare and threw it back at him. 'I used to think somebody might, Stan, but nobody ever did.' He turned back to the pan and stirred it violently. I imagined him doing the same every night and my anger subsided. 'Farm keeps you busy, I suppose?'

'Aye. Aye, it does, and there's no harm in that.'

'We were sorry to hear about Joyce, in Australia,' I said. Stan turned and stared in frank scepticism at this. 'Okay, so Dad rang once to tell me and he didn't really seem to give a fuck. Happy now?'

Stan raised the pewter spoon, dripping with sauce, and waved it threateningly at me, then let a cracked smoker's laugh escape. 'Happy? Yeah, happy as Larry, lad.' Still he laughed, but quietly now, with a wheeze which turned to a cough.

I watched orange sauce collecting over the stone floor.

'Well, I mean, it's not that nobody cares, Stan, but they've all got their own lives —' I recalled his movements across the field earlier. 'What about you? Are you okay living on your own? I suppose there are compensations — like eating whatever crap you want, eh?'

Stan's smile vanished as he took the pan off the stove. 'Not a lot. Look, lad, I don't know what y' doin' here on your lonesome, without your fiancée, but I hope you're not looking for some bachelor's paradise, because I hate beans, I hate this sodden bloody hill, and for your information Joyce was a bloody wonderful cook when she put her mind to it.'

I shut up then, and sat down while Stan poured dinner all over two plates. Sitting down wearily at the table against the wall, he put his hand briefly on my shoulder and gave it a little squeeze. 'Here y' are,' he said, as if it meant something.

Over the table, stuck to the wall with Sellotape, was an old Ordnance Survey map. 'Does that cover this whole area?' I asked. 'Where's that monument I saw up there?'

'Goodley Pike? Is that what you're after: the Pike?' Stan tapped a spot on the map with his fork. 'Tallest point for fifty mile,' he said.

With my finger, I traced the dotted lines leading north, east and south from the Pike. 'They're footpaths, are they?'

'Paths, aye. Or used to be. Half of them'd be overgrown by now. No one walks to Whinely or Soppstone any more. Except those bloody Scandinavians, if they zig when they should zag, looking for William bloody Shakespeare's birthplace, or some such.'

'Soppstone? Where's that?'

'There, south. An hour's walk at most. Folk up here'd hardly blink at that, years back.'

Stan found a couple of beers and mentioned England versus Italy on telly. We might even have spent the rest of the night in companionable depression, if the beer hadn't compelled me to drag up the past. 'Just tell me, Stan: did you know straightaway, back when Mum died? I bet Dad never called you, did he?'

Stan didn't look too pleased at this line of questioning, but he didn't look surprised either. 'I believe he called Alice. Alice rang, at any rate. We knew right enough.' He went to the sink with his plate.

'So you didn't think to fly over, or at least write or something? I thought you and Alice were supposed to be close to Mum.'

'Oy! Y' can cut that out,' Stan said, loud and sharp. 'Supposed to be what? Finish up, will you, so I can clear up. I can break in next door if I want to spend all night being questioned about my activities, but I've no desire. Here: y' can lend a hand.' He threw me a dishcloth. It was wet. I threw it back.

'If you say nowt, I'll know nowt,' I said.

Stan picked up the dishcloth, glanced sadly my way and turned on the hot water.

I lay awake for a long time, listening to the wind building and falling. It had blown away the cloud, and moonlight now cut a path across the room below. I tried to guess the time, sensing it was morning in Fremantle. I felt the bed shift as Vanessa rose for work, then underfoot the cool crust of beach sand breaking, giving way to the warmer, softer sand underneath.

I had to climb downstairs to close the shutters against the moon. Outside, I could see a black fold, south of the Pike. I retraced in my mind the broken lines crossing contours on the old map. One phone call and I'd know where to go. I could already feel the land rising and falling under my feet in waves.

# II

The weather had cleared by the time I stepped out into the yard late next morning. I could see signs of neglect that I'd missed the previous afternoon: rusting tools and weeds in the yard, fallen sections of drystone walls around the adjoining field. I kicked tentatively at loose stone and another section fell with a soft thud, swallowed by long grass on the far side. I looked back in alarm but Stan's door was shut, with no signs of life. In the opposite direction I could see the Pike very clearly against the pale sky.

Without a map there wasn't much point to heading up there yet. I felt a bit pathetic now anyway, cowering in my corner like an old man harbouring grudges, so I walked over to Stan's door. No one answered my knock. The door was unlocked. I called his name but got no reply. Treading carefully, I moved into the hall and found the phone. I tried the Soppstone number but it just kept ringing, so I went looking for Stan.

I found him behind the garage with his arse in a pool of mud and his back against the stone wall. He was asleep, with his mouth open and his neck bent awkwardly back and to one side. He had a huge overcoat on that might once have been Joyce's. The fur collar was up and one hand was gripping it tight like it was a blanket.

I couldn't see any bottles about, but the back door to the garage was wide open and the light was on. I shook Stan gently and he made prehistoric noises, but he couldn't open his eyes. His face was very pale. I had to heave him to his feet and throw his arm over me. He turned out to be surprisingly light: I was able to take him in through the back door to the kitchen easily. I grabbed a tea towel as I went and sat his muddy arse on that, in what looked like his favourite armchair. He suffered me to pat down his halo of white hair, then he started to shiver, so I found a blanket and put that over him.

He didn't look so frightening any more. 'You haven't been out there all night, have you Stan?' He raised an eyebrow a little, and I knew it was true. 'You can't stay like this,' I said. 'You're a bit wet, mate. You need to warm up. A bath, really. All right, Stan? Take a bath, eh? Can you manage that y'self?' Again the brow-wrinkling thing, more ironic this time. 'No? Bloody hell.' I looked towards the hall as if the nurse had come in, but we were it. 'Who's your doctor?'

Stan stirred at this. His eyes opened a little. 'Nay, lad,' he murmured, and he sounded scared.

I hesitated, thinking of finding a hospital, then went and ran a bath instead. 'All right,' I said, 'but you'll have to help.'

I leant him against the bathroom wall while I pulled his clothes off. Lumps of wet clay fell off onto the tiles with the pants. His body was very lean and hard, but the skin was loose and he was shaking violently by the time he lowered himself into the water, hanging on my arm. As the warmth soaked in, his face reddened slowly and he closed his eyes. I stood by the door watching him until a voice rose from the dead, slow and low: 'All right, lad. Show's over. See to the chickens.' I hesitated. 'Go on. I won't drown,' he said, and he closed his eyes again.

Outside, the wind had settled down and there was a high seamless blanket of cloud. It was sheltered down there, and the air was oddly mild for February. That's what had saved Stan probably — that and all those long nights on guard with a torch and a thermos.

I found some feed and threw it at the chooks in their filthy little pen. They didn't throw it back so I guess they were happy enough. All I could think of was Stan's face, and his skinny white body. His face was scarred, I realised now, not just old: there were marks of collapse under his right eye, some subsidence of the heart I knew nothing about, which had left a permanent purple mark and a sceptical squint.

I had vague memories of a younger Stan, with a slick black wave of hair, thicker and bouncier, and a sharp face you'd want to look at but not trust. I'd never really known Stan but my father's contempt still pained me. The best I ever heard was 'Joyce could have done worse' or 'He stuck by her at least, when all's said and done.' That sort of thing.

I went back in and watched Stan struggling out of the bath, until he told me to bugger off. In the kitchen I made a stew using what I could find. There were vegetables after all — even split peas, which might have been there for years. While it boiled, I settled Stan down in front of telly in the lounge and dragged out his little heater. Then I went back to the kitchen and eased the Ordnance Survey map off the wall as quietly as I could. It folded neatly into my jacket pocket. A little later, I took him in his soup. We sat there watching football and eating without a word. When he stopped eating I took the bowl back and he dozed off.

I stepped lightly into the hall and swallowed hard. Then I took a deep breath and rang Vanessa in Perth.

'You're not being very funny,' she said, when I told her where I was. Then, after a moment's silence, she sounded scared. 'You're not really in England?'

'It looked like Bombay when I arrived, I admit, but all the signs said Manchester. Unless I find a lot of linen for sale, I'm assuming this is it.'

'You're still not being funny,' she said in her warning tone. 'I can't believe this. You'll be trying to explain this for the rest of your career.'

'Oh, I think that bridge might be well and truly burned, by now. Bloody hope so. It's no great loss, V. One job in commercial law is much like another, in Perth.'

'You're forgetting one minor detail, aren't you: that bit about us getting married, remember?'

'That's a year away yet.' The response to this was a big nothing, but what could I say: that three days away and I was already wondering why I'd proposed? That I felt awake at last, that a spell over me seemed to be breaking? The wind whistled like a warning at the foot of the front door, and I could hear Stan from the parlour, rumbling and groaning in his sleep like a wounded bear. 'This is just a chance to catch up with family,' I said.

'Bit late for that, isn't it? You've shown no interest before. You wouldn't even have a drink with your dad.'

'I'm not talking about him, am I? I mean those I left behind.'

'Oh, for Christ's sake, George! You weren't rescued from a war zone were you? You emigrated, that's all. What's the big deal? I just don't get it. Why couldn't you have waited?'

'You would have talked me out of it.'

'Oh, I wouldn't have dreamed of talking you out of running away from your work and your wedding and everything you've ever had, on some childish impulse, just when your job was on the line. That would have been terrible, George, if I'd talked you out of that.'

'Two weeks, V. Max. Then we carry on as planned.'

'Bastard.'

'Yes, I'm a bastard.' I heard a sigh at the other end, then a keyboard tapping angrily. 'I'm staying with my Uncle Stan. He's got a spare cottage. Dad mentioned it years ago, remember?'

'He called it a shed.'

'Yeah; a try-hard snob like my dad would.'

'You really are a bastard.'

'I'll call again when I —'

'Bastard.' She hung up. Thank God.

I pulled out the page from the directory then and tried the last number. This time it was engaged, which meant someone lived there at least. Worth a walk, then.

I went back and watched the end of the football, then I turned it off and woke Stan. 'I'm off,' I said. 'You should get off to bed.'

'So?' Stan said, when I tried to move him.

'You'll be all right now I think, Stan.'

'No. For God's sake: did we win?'

'Oh. Yes. I mean, no, I don't think so.'

'You don't think so? Bloody Nora. Neither of us know, then, do we? I'll have to call Bob and see.' He seemed in danger of nodding off again, so I led him to bed.

Patting the map in my pocket, I set off quickly down the road the way I'd first come. At the T-junction a walled lane headed uphill, under an arch of shaken trees. Past the last house the gusts grew stronger, and angrier again after the last field, where rocks broke through the grass. I was light-headed by then, and gasping for breath, the hill was so steep. The gale was almost lifting me up from rock to rock as I climbed.

The Pike itself was massive, close up. The shaft stood on a square base of dark stone as tall as a double-storey house. I walked around to the south side, where the hilltop swept away to a low brow of short grasses littered with bare stone. I could see what looked like trails meandering away out of sight, crossing each other in places as they went. I was getting punch-drunk from the gale coming across the valley, so I moved in between two square buttresses where pools of water lay shivering.

There was an arched opening in the wall there with stone steps spiralling up into blackness. Suspecting a viewing platform atop the base, I stepped over the pools and crossed the dark threshold. The wind made a low turbine sound against the rough circular hub at the centre of the stair. The stone seemed to vibrate, as if generating the wind itself. I felt my way on up in the dark and found a narrow open terrace running around the column, high enough to see in every direction. I could see a deep valley to the west, where light was falling in sheets like a storm, picking out streaks of green amongst the broad sheen. To the north, enormous white wind turbines littered a high plateau and to the south and east tracks wound away over open moorland, through wind-driven waves of grass that seemed to pour up the slopes.

I got Stan's map out and spread it on the floor in the shelter of the parapet, orientating it as best I could with the hills around. The lines in the grass started to make sense, and in the far south I could see the guidance I'd sought: three houses close together on the third rise. Backfold Lane.

I shot back down the stairs and leapt on across the wet grass towards the south, feeling purposeful at last, with the luminous grey sky so broad before me. It was as if I had a path again after years of wandering, a path back to where I'd once been. I followed the narrow trail of bare black earth down the hillside until it crossed a shallow ford and split into two on the far rise. The map tore badly when I pulled it out in the wind. It directed me to the right, but the slope was steep and it wasn't long before I had to stop to get my breath. The light was fading now, so I set off again straightaway, determined not to turn back.

The next valley was deeper, with walled fields on either side and a line of bare trees along the stream. Sheep were sheltering at the base of the low stone walls, their green eyes watching me pass. There was more water about by then and the light was getting poor, so I slowed and took care where I trod, choosing my crossing carefully at the stream.

I lost the path on the far side, which rose steeply to broken terraces of slippery black stone, forcing me onto my hands. Gaining the ridge, I could see a narrow walled lane below, running flat between high open moorland and fields on the lower side. A hundred yards or so down this lane, three stone houses stood facing the valley, with small yards backing onto the lane. The first house was dark and looked neglected. The second had lost its roof altogether and much of its back walls. The third house was intact, and showed light at a window on the upper floor, facing the lane.

I had to negotiate a way down through boggy ground, and over a couple of high stiles. It was almost dark by the time I jumped down onto the hard surface of the lane. Far away on the other side of the valley were house and street lights and the softer glow of Soppstone itself.

The wind dropped entirely as I reached the ruined house, and I heard the peculiar sound the world makes when nothing is moving, like the sound in your head just before sleep. Then a little gust sent all the deep shadows of the open house humming mournfully around me.

I came up to the third house, where the one light upstairs had stayed on. All I could see there was a white rectangle of ceiling. There was no gate into the back yard, so I climbed the low wall bordering the lane, making the coping stones rock. I crossed the yard towards the house, the sound of long grass trailing against my jeans. As I came close to the back door, full moonlight came out above the slate eaves like a searchlight.

The stone walls of the house before me seemed to grow in that light, and I felt the house as a living thing seated there. I felt its size, its weight, its depths and hidden places. I imagined it in sunshine and in rain over the years. I saw it almost crack with cold in the snow. I felt its secret damp, its tired timbers, its claustrophobic hold on those inside.

The moon faded again, but another light hit out from the window before me, and I was afraid to move for fear of being seen. There was a kitchen framed before me suddenly, with yellow walls and a bare light bulb, and there was Kate walking into it.

# III

I'd forgotten how small she was. She'd filled out a little, and cut her hair shoulder-length, yet essentially she was just the same as the last time I'd seen her — eerily so. Watching her was remembering her — even her movements as she put a big black kettle on the stove and paused there, with her cheek in her palm. That used to puzzle me enormously, that pose: it suggested mysteries I couldn't fathom. How right I'd been.

Taking up thoughts suspended a decade ago, I wondered anew at her strange, vaguely Eastern face, her thick black hair. Why was she so dark and odd, if her parents were just Londoners? Maybe she was part Jewish, or Polish, or Mongolian for all I knew. What she was that night was worried, I could tell, though she had the kind of face that always looked worried. She even had a worried laugh. But tonight she was worried, and she wasn't laughing. She even looked a little pale, in that harsh light.

She looked up as I watched, hearing something upstairs perhaps, and she turned off the stove and walked out of sight. I took a couple of steps closer, as if to follow her, and stared at the spot where she'd been. I was close enough now to be lit by the window: if she came back she'd see me, I knew. I couldn't let that happen, but something made me stay. Then I heard something that drew me even closer: the high voice of a boy, coming down from the upper floor.

'I want you to promise!'

Before thinking, I was walking up, opening the back door and stepping into the old scullery. Dirty Wellingtons were strewn across the floor, and I had to tiptoe through them in the dark, towards the half-open door at the far end. Glancing back I could see moonlit sheep through the open back door, phosphorescent in the dark.

'Promise!'

Definitely a boy. Eight years old? Ten? I let myself down off my toes. There was light in the passage beyond, with cheap botanic prints on the wall. I could hear faint sounds of movement above, and Kate's voice, very blurred and low.

She was alone in the house with the boy, I could tell. I opened the door a little and stepped into the hall. Shavings of mud fell over the carpet at my feet, and I had to crouch down and throw them back into the scullery. To my left was the kitchen: I could see old timber cupboards, with aluminium pans hanging overhead. To my right, the hall led to a carpeted stair. I stepped lightly down the hall, keeping to a narrow red rug that ran its length, until I could see up the steps to a landing. Kate's voice was clearer now.

'If there were any way for me to do that, love, I'd do it,' she was saying in a conciliatory tone. 'But Vic won't have it, I know that, without askin'. You'll have to make do.'

'No harm in askin',' said the boy.

'I don't want to upset him. You know what he's like. It's not worth the grief.'

'I don't care.'

'That's not true. What's the matter with you?' Silence. 'Come on, get yourself dry. You know he loves you.'

'No, I don't.'

'Tom. That's enough. Dry and bed.'

A door opened and there were footsteps overhead. I got back into the scullery fast and hurried outdoors, closing the door gently after me. On the edge of the flagstones, half-crouched as if ready to run, I waited. It seemed much colder than before and I started to shake, pulling my jacket tight around me and fumbling with the buttons. The upstairs light went off overhead, but the kitchen light stayed on, with no sign of Kate. I stepped further away, back into the grass, and circled a little to the left to see what more of the house was visible, but could see nothing new, with the other lights off. Was she having tea or not? Why had she left the light on, if she'd stayed upstairs? Was she expecting someone? I tried sitting on the wall along the lane and waiting but the cold got to me.

It wasn't easy finding my way back up to the path I'd come by. When I got up there, I found a sort of trail, but still wasn't sure it was the right one until the first stream gave me my bearings again. The queer thing was that Kate hadn't looked any different. She should have looked like someone else by now.

The grasses moved angrily around me. Twice I stopped and looked back for the light I'd stood under, amongst the little constellation fringing the valley there, but I couldn't tell one from another. The way seemed darker than ever. At my feet, trails constantly diverged and multiplied, but it was too dim and too late to consult the map so I stopped looking and trusted in my instincts to get me back. Soon the Pike started to appear over each rise, larger each time, leading me back.

As I passed it, coming over the last rise, I looked up. The moon was out, silhouetting the black mass, and making it look bigger than ever. Its tip was precise, as if built that day, only sharpened and hardened by the thousands of miserable wet nights it had spent out there. It was as if I'd stumbled into a place where time changed nothing. Kate was still there, after all those years. I could even speak to her, if I dared. And the boy? There at least was change.

By the time my feet hit tarmac at the end of Stan's road, I was thinking only of the bed at the top of the ladder, and reminding myself to close the shutters. But there was a red van in the yard that I hadn't seen before. Its engine was running and its tail-lights were on, glowing like coals in a red mist of exhaust fumes. I nearly walked past before I realised Stan was peering out of the passenger window. 'George? What the bleeding hell are you doing out?' he demanded.

'Me? I saw you to bed hours ago. Where've you been in this?'

'Excuse me, Mother. Beg yours, I'm sure. I've just been up to the pub on the Tops with Bob for a quick 'un, since you ask. We've come back for a bit of a top-up.'

'So what are you doing in there?'

'Don't rightly know,' he said, staring at the empty driver's seat. I opened his door, and he exited in a controlled tumble. 'I thought you'd want to meet Bob.'

Against the wall of the garage we found the silhouette of a tall, thin man spreadeagled like a captured escapee.

'All right then, Bob?' Stan asked in a soft voice. He put his hand on the man's shoulder and led him inside. Bob plonked himself down in an armchair while Stan dragged out his pitiful little two-bar heater and put it just beyond range. He turned one bar on and set to rattling glasses and bottles in the sideboard.

Bob sat slumped into the folds of his filthy green parka, with his head resting on one huge hand. He had a lot of hair which didn't sweep or fall — it just hovered there like a halo, making him look even taller. There was the beginning of a beard too and heavy black eyebrows over his closed eyes. When Stan handed him a glass, he opened his eyes and gingerly peered down at the brown liquid before sipping. Then he groaned as if to comfort himself with the sound and turned his eyes on me.

'Gooday,' he said, northern vowels attached. He was looking at me suspiciously I thought, but that might have been a hangover from the way he looked at his drink. Or it might just have been a hangover. Stan was banging doors in the kitchen.

'George,' I said. 'George Fielden.' I offered Bob my hand and he grabbed it like he was falling.

'Bob Gallagher,' he said with gathering cheer. 'Are you Stan's nephew? You look just like him.'

'Thanks. How do you know him?'

'Work, years back. I'm an electrician,' he said and immediately looked like he wanted to change the subject. He took a swig at his drink and shuddered extravagantly. He was so big that the armchair shuddered too.

Stan came in bearing a modicum of nuts and sat beside me on the sofa. Vapours of whisky and chicken shit swarmed alluringly around him. 'Don't do much of anything these days, eh Bob?' he said.

'Had a job down Shaw way last week,' Bob said defensively.

'Light bulb gone again?' Stan enquired, then leant over with the whisky bottle and refilled my glass, then Bob's, christening Bob's jeans too for good measure.

Bob turned a little grey once his glass was empty again. 'A bit of air,' Stan suggested, and shepherded him through the kitchen to the back door. Stan came back alone and adopted a confidential tone. 'He's got digs in Rochdale, poor bugger: one of those flats near Milnrow. His missus threw him out three year ago, and she's buggered off to God knows where, so he's got no way of seeing his Lucy now. She were a bonny un too, that Lucy.'

'He has a daughter? Can't he trace her?'

'Oh, I think they're down Cheshire way,' Stan said with finality.

'So? It's not the moon.'

'There's no way Bob's traipsin' halfway round bloody Cheshire: I can tell y' that for nowt.'

'So how do you know him?'

'From Cheapgard. Bob used to fix alarms for 'em but he lost the contract. It were the booze behind that, same as with the wife. I try to help as I can but what can y' do?' He raised his hands helplessly, refilled Bob's glass to the brim and as Bob came clumping back, passed it to him. 'Health,' he said.

'Stan said you're staying in Rochdale.'

Recognising that an explanation was required, Bob nodded grimly. 'Born there. I'll die there too, at this rate.'

'Bob applied to emigrate,' Stan said. 'He was turned down.'

'Thanks, Stan. Like, I really wanted George to know that.'

'There's nowt to be ashamed of, lad. You're still good enough for England.'

I laughed then and they both looked at me in surprise. 'But why Australia?' I asked. 'Why leave the country?'

'I'd have thought you'd know, coming from there. I mean, it's worth a hundred bloody Birminghams, in't it?'

'A lot you'd know about it,' Stan said, and turned to me. 'He's never been south of Sheffield, that one.'

'So? I've seen enough bloody television, haven't I?'

'But Stan says you have a daughter here.'

'Does he now?' Bob glared at the old man.

'You'd want to stay for her sake, wouldn't you?' I persisted. 'Or would she have gone with you?'

'Yeah, right. I wish. In my dreams, maybe. Lucy's all right in bloody Cheshire, I'm told. Perfectly all right and in no need of me, thank you very much. I like to think, George, that I'm just the right man in the wrong place, you know? Maybe in Australia I could have been a success, you know, like Burke and Wills, or Ned Kelly or someone famous.'

'They died, Bob.'

He nodded sombrely, not listening. 'But here — you've no bloody hope here. It's just too bloody hard.'

'Typical,' Stan muttered.

'What's that supposed to mean: "Typical"? I suppose you like it here, Mister Bloody Gentleman Farmer, eh?'

'Not for me to like,' Stan said, flat and final. 'This is it, in't it? There's no bloody point goin' on about it. You've made your bed ...'

'That's all you bloody say. Is it so bad to want a couple of weeks on a beach and a glimpse of the miserable sun? Is that too much to ask?'

'It is Lucy,' Stan assured me confidentially, as if Bob weren't there.

'Lucy has nowt to do with either of you,' Bob said. 'Me neither, if I'm honest. Me neither.'

'Oh cheer up, for God's sake!' Stan said. 'We beat Italy didn't we? What more do you want?'

Bob raised his soggy head at this and produced a boyish grin. 'I reckon that'll do me for the next twenty year,' he said and laughed. 'Did you see that bloody Maldini's face when he saw the linesman with his bloody arm down?'

'I only hope we paid that linesman enough,' Stan said, and they laughed together, any rancour between them evaporating in the face of home team support. I left them half an hour later, still emptying whisky down their throats and still talking football, the best friends in the world.

# IV

There was a new sharpness in the air when I emerged next day, and the cold seemed to be tightening its grip even as I stood in the yard. It was a reminder that winter wasn't over, that in a sense it never was. Things needn't necessarily get better, ever. I let the cold dampen the crazy hope I felt stirring in my breast whenever I thought of Kate and the path over the hill to her door. I could no more knock on that door than fly to the moon, but it was becoming a struggle to believe it. It seemed so close, suddenly: as close as yesterday.

What I should really be doing, I knew, was contacting Vanessa. She didn't have my number, so she'd expect me to call again. But the time difference conspired with thoughts of Kate to paralyse me for a day or two, and I found myself helping Stan on the farm instead.

Over the next couple of days the cold deepened, until field and stone stood frozen in hard frost each morning.

Lines of clear ice started to form along the tiny shores of drains in the shadows of the stone walls. I helped Stan take in the sheep and patch up the walls in the more sheltered fields behind the barns. Against all expectations Stan proved excellent company — perhaps because he didn't say much. I happily took his cue, watching and learning and keeping my mouth shut most of the time. I found I enjoyed the work, even enjoyed the cold, which in turn kept me working. It was only when I looked up and saw more work waiting in every direction that I felt tiredness creep in and wondered at Stan surviving up there on his lonesome with his dodgy back and his broken heart.

Eventually I had to ask, 'Why are we doing this, Stan?' He looked annoyed but I could tell he knew what I meant. 'I realise we're keeping the sheep in and that's got to be done, and if they stay over that side you'll lose them, but why have the sheep in the first place? You can't make much money out of them.'

'A lot you'd know about it.' He weighed the stone in his hand and looked over the wall to the empty field beyond, still coated with frost halfway through the morning. 'Used to make a bit, selling lambs in autumn to farms lower down,' he said. 'That was in Arthur's day.'

'Your uncle?'

'Aye. The one that left me this mess. And he was a bugger for getting subsidies, too. Had more subsidies for this one miserable bloody farm than half of Scotland in the end. I can't be bothered with all that.'

'So why the sheep?'

'I like 'em.' He didn't look the least bit bashful, saying this. He placed the stone carefully and took a look uphill towards the new estate. 'I like 'em a damn sight more than all the shoddy bloody subdivisions and Ye Olde Tea Shoppes sprouting everywhere else, at any road.'

'There must be ways to make money off land like this. What about around Soppstone? There's plenty of farms over that way — some of them must make a living.'

'They're all on the dole.'

'But some of those Soppstone farms seem to be working.'

'What's so fascinating about bleeding Soppstone? Look lad, the land's just not good enough for this new market they all talk about.'

'They have farms on worse land in Australia.'

'Yes lad, but I don't happen to have a million bloody acres here, if you haven't noticed. Oh, I dare say there's ways — y' can tear down all these walls easy enough, and folk even talk about plantations and deer, for God's sake. It'll be tigers next. I can't be bothered with all that. I'm too old. It'd take someone younger.' Stan most decidedly did not look at me, saying this, and got back to work.

It took a few mornings, but eventually I got up in time to see Stan emerge on his first rounds outside. Calculating, I realised it was an ideal time to call Vanessa, so I stomped reluctantly over to Stan's house, kicking at the gravel like a schoolboy.

Her voice was softer than I remembered it. She sounded tired, so I asked if she'd had a hard day.

'Harder than yours, I dare say.'

'I haven't had it yet. It's morning here. We're going shopping on Wednesday.'

'Wow, George! Wonderful! That's one thing you can't do in Australia!'

'Come on, Vanessa: it's been really good so far. I've been working with my Uncle Stan on the farm.'

'You sound about ten years old, you know that, don't you? You sound like you're calling from Famous Five Have Fun.'

I laughed and after a reluctant pause she laughed too. 'Feels odd,' I admitted. 'Being here, hearing you. Feels like it's years since I left.'

'You seem to be taking the whole thing terribly seriously for a fortnight's holiday. When's your flight back, anyway?'

This was the tricky part. 'Haven't actually booked one yet. I wasn't sure how long I'd be. I thought maybe ...' I swallowed hard,' maybe a month would be right. Make the most of the ticket. It's working out well here, with Stan and everything, so ...' I trailed off lamely.

There was silence for a moment. 'What's going on?' she said quietly. 'Why am I suddenly the high school girlfriend hanging out for a date?'

'I don't know what you're talking about. I just want —'

'No. Don't tell me what you want — as long as you know. I'll just hang around and wait for a call, shall I? Except it doesn't work that way, does it? What happens is you finally ring me when you feel like it and I tell you to go to hell.'

She hung up in fine style, and all I felt was relief. My thoughts drifted to Kate again, and the life I might have led. I couldn't resist any longer. I had to know more. I had to know how mad it was to hope after all these years, after all I'd done. But as I headed out to the yard with the walk to Soppstone in mind, Stan was already there waiting for me, hands on hips like a one-man picket line. 'She'll be missing you, I suppose?' he ventured.

'Who?'

'Who'd y' bloody think?'

'Vanessa? Oh, in her own fashion,' I said. 'She'll have no one to argue with when she comes home. She'll miss me then. Nothing makes Vanessa angrier than having no one to argue with.'

'And? So?' He hadn't moved and he was looking very expectantly at me.

'So: when are you goin' back?' He seemed particularly cold and stern saying this, but something made me disbelieve it.

'If I'm in the road here just say so.'

'You know it's not that, lad. You've been a right help. As long as it's all right with folk on that side.' He nodded vaguely southward.

'What folk? There's no folk. You've no bloody idea, Stan.'

'But y' don't belong here, lad. Y' should be with y' missus.'

'There's no missus, either. Jesus, Stan! Where've you been the last hundred years?'

'I might ask you the same question, if we're honest.

But I won't. I'll only ask again when you plan to go.'

'I might stay yet,' I said. 'I might not go back at all. Who knows?'

This was such clear evidence of insanity that Stan just nodded grimly like a doctor at a fatal x-ray, and walked back to the garage. There was a slow, sharp breeze picking up from the west. I stood there staring up at the Tops. Soon I could hear Stan whistling 'Sally' in the garage. I was still thinking of Kate, of course. Knowing Stan was completely right wasn't going to stop me.

It was so gloomy as I struggled up the hillside that I didn't even notice the first snow fall. Only when I reached the peak, with the tip of the Pike lost in a white stream, did I realise how the whole valley had sunk under an opaque blanket. The sky itself seemed to be closing in.

I brushed the snow from my shoulders and shoved wet hands into my jacket pockets. The map, I now realised, was still in sodden halves beside the bed. I should go back down, I thought, I don't really know the way, not for sure. But instead I watched the sea of cloud dip and sweep over the silver valleys, and I felt my heart open up and let in the country. There was no going back now: I was at the world's centre again. I was home, and no harm could come to me while I stayed. I had this obscure hope, nudging me on over the hill like a gale — this hope that I fitted in here somehow after all. Maybe I could speak to Kate. Maybe I could stay with Stan … Possibilities started to lurk in the obscure distances ahead.

So I walked, along a path I thought I might have

known all along, and as I walked the sky brightened and then dimmed again, but the snow kept coming in, sometimes fast across my path, sometimes only drifting. Finding the lane was easier in daylight, despite the snow, but I had to approach the houses with more care, not wanting to be seen. I stopped beside the neighbouring ruin and leant against the rear wall, which had crumbled away to head height, forcing me to bend my knees a little and hide like a fugitive. Somehow all my brave, insane resolutions to knock on Kate's door had already melted away.

Snow kept drifting in against the dark stone, collecting along the foot of the drystone walls and on the roof of Kate's house next door, catching under the slates, but melting clear around the smoking chimney. The smoke was curling up and getting tangled in a gathering gale from the west. The walls around me started to emit a long, low warning tone. I heard a deeper bass note too, that seemed to rise from some cavern or cellar under my feet like a growl. I began to wonder at the wisdom of being there in such weather, or to be more accurate, I began to think myself an idiot to be cowering there at all.

Then I looked again through the old window opening and I saw him for the first time.

The boy was smaller than I'd imagined, with a mop of scraggly dark hair blowing over his neck and face. He had on a red anorak which caught the wind, ballooning and spinning around him loosely as if there wasn't much inside. I thought he was dancing at first. He was moving back and forth, going nowhere, and feinting with his arms down like an armless boxer. Then he bent low and tapped the air sideways with his shoe and I recognised the gesture: a shot for goal from a tight angle, at close range. He was playing football.

Except he didn't have one.

I might have thought him mad, dodging and dancing about in the snow like that on his own, if I hadn't done the same thing myself years before. The memory of similar mornings flooded back. I had to move away from the window. I sat down, tucking my jacket under me on the wet stone and staring at the bare wall opposite, trying to calm down. I didn't even know what upset me so much. There were just these waves of snow leaping in over the walls, wetting my jeans, slapping my face, and each one was like a horrible, bottomless wave of sorrow and shame. I knew I couldn't talk to the boy, but I couldn't just go, either. Not now. The floor and the walls groaned as if tired of hiding me.

When I looked again he'd lost his invisible ball. He had his hood up and was staring past the house, down the hill. Over the wind I could hear it too: a car engine, grumbling up the slope towards us, the sound blown up by the wind and bouncing off the clouds. Then a black car bonnet emerged north of the house and the boy spoke, the wind carrying it across to where I hid. He said 'When you don't know, you are afraid.'

I didn't believe it at first, it sounded so strange. Then, as the car glided slowly up, the boy darted away behind the house. He paused at the back door, shook his hood back off his head and looked up and around at the sky, as if unnerved. I saw a pale, round face, then he stamped his boots hard on the porch step and hurried in.

The car was an old Zephyr, of all things, all black and chrome like something out of Z-Cars, and the man who emerged was perfectly cast as the villain. He wasn't particularly tall — perhaps my height — but he wore a loose black jacket which made him look bigger, and it was far too stylish anyway. Evidence of some kind of grim vanity. Flash, Stan'd call it.

I got a look at his profile as he walked across to the house: dark hair cropped fashionably short, like a murderer, so the scalp showed through. Full cheeks, prone to fat. Blank dark eyes.

He walked very quickly to the front door, without looking around. I had to suppress an impulse to call out. God knows what. I just hated to hide from that man. He opened the front door and went straight in, as if he owned the place. For all I knew, he did.

I scrambled out and walked down the lane, stopping under the tree. Through the kitchen window I could see the same yellow walls as before and Kate again, with her back against the bench and her hair tied back like she'd often had it when she was younger, except this time it was in the hands of someone else. Someone in a wide black jacket had one hand behind her head, his fingers buried in her dark hair, pulling out the tie. In his other hand he held her chin like a china cup, and he was leaning over to drink, pushing her up against the bench. Her eyes were closed.

That was enough. I should have gone then, but I stayed just that little too long, mesmerised by what I saw as the man reached under Kate's woollen top and moved his hand slowly over her breast, up and over until her mouth opened a little. I watched this and felt something so horribly close to excitement that I knew I could never, ever admit to being there and watching.

I turned back down the lane in a hurry, slipping on patches of black ice. I climbed up out of the lane and stomped uphill, making a mess of the fresh crust of snow, angry with myself. I took the stile quickly, pulled up my collar and tramped on, wondering despite myself about the boy. Where had he gone, while they …?

It didn't matter. Not to me, anyway. I'd had my questions answered. The boy had a father. I wouldn't be coming back.

I stopped and took a good look around me. Only short black walls and the skeleton of an occasional tree broke through the snow. Less and less was left to guide me. Further ahead to my left I could just see a line of taller trees and at their base black reeds marking a stream. But I was far from lost and the fact only dismayed me. The Pike would appear soon enough, I knew, and beyond that I could be on a plane in a few days time, if I paid enough. With a bit of judicious flattery I could be back at work within the week, as if nothing had happened: secrets intact, questions answered, no one hurt.

So of course I felt like shit.

And all the time I could only think of the boy pausing on his back step, gazing around at a big, blank world.

He just looked so small, darting his head about nervously like that. The trails of snow circling him must have been a hundred or a thousand times his height.

# V

'Tell you what, Vanessa: let's get married as soon as we can.'

Vanessa's most satanic laugh came over the line. 'You're serious, aren't you? Why the big rush, all of a sudden? What's the matter? You sound upset.'

'Nothing a brandy couldn't fix.'

'What time is it over there? I thought it was morning.'

'No, no: it's cocktail hour over here.' I surveyed the dark and ruined interior of Stan's parlour through the open doorway. I could see an empty bottle by the armchair, keeping an empty glass company. 'The party never ends, up at Stan's Piano Bar,' I said.

'Not having fun any more, up on Mystery Moor?'

'It's more like Five Get Thoroughly Pissed-Off Miles From A Decent Restaurant, actually.'

'But you knew that before you went. You've said it all a thousand times, about what a dump you came from, and how awful your family were, and so on. That's what was so weird about you rushing off like that. You never even said you wanted to go back there.'

'I was like — you know what I was like? I was like the bloke who's left his packet of fags in a minefield and keeps thinking about them. He knows it's mad, but he keeps thinking about that packet, about those cigarettes he's never smoked, and he wants to go back. He's given up smoking even, and still he's picturing that packet out there, deep in the minefield, well out of bounds.'

'You know of course that I haven't a clue what you're talking about? I'm supposed to be working, George. Remember that: work? What am I going to put in my logbook: fags in a minefield?'

'I just feel like I've stuffed you around a bit, that's all. I want to make up, get married, sort it out.'

'Wow. A speech. And this revelation has come to you because ...?'

'Because if you can make something up and do the right thing, you should. And if you can't ... well, you don't.'

'Right. Hard to argue with that, George dear, but is more coming?'

'Sorry?'

'What's happened, George? Just tell me what's happened to bring on all this inspirational verse. And please don't tell me you're born again.'

'Look, I didn't think wanting to get married sooner would start an argument.'

'All right, all right. Don't sulk. You just sound so

different. Is it so terrible of me to want you back?' Her tone had changed, the sarcasm was gone, and I could see her clearly suddenly — the flecks of jade in her candid eyes, the sadness that was all too real. It was like I'd never been away. I wanted that, momentarily — wanted the certainty of that. She needed me there — the fact was newly solid before me, yet I still didn't know what to say.

'George? Are you there, George?'

'Yes, V. Sorry.' And I was sorry, saying it — more sorry than I could let her know. 'Look, I'll book a flight today. I'm going into town. Bob helps out with a kids' football team, and he's asked me along.'

'Wow.'

'Don't knock it,' I said. 'This is a big day for me. I'm Going Out.'

Most of the night's snowfall had melted by the time Bob eased his van down Soppstone's main road. The town looked rather sodden, but comfortably placed along the canal all the same, with stone terraces stepping improbably up some of the steeper slopes to where the white moors circled around. As we drove around the corner, past the huge classical town hall, the gutters were running fast with melted snow. Under the high dripping arches of the railway viaduct a few market stalls cowered.

'Football first,' I said. 'I'll do the travel agent after.'

There was a stiff breeze blowing down the valley, making the gutters sparkle. 'When do you go back, then?' Bob asked.

'Not you, as well! That's all anyone wants to know: when am I buggering off.'

'I suppose you seem a bit out of place. The thing is, George: no one comes back, as a rule, except to rubbish the place.' He drove on thoughtfully for a second, speeding up the wipers as the rain set in.

'Can't think why,' I said, and we both laughed.

Before we reached the centre of Whinely, Bob turned left through a narrow gap between terraces and pulled in beside a sign announcing ABATTOIR PARK.

'There used to be an abattoir here, I suppose?'

Bob shook his head, puzzled. 'No,' he said. 'Not that I know of.' He rubbed his hands with glee. 'There's nothin' like it, though, is there? What a lark, eh?'

I looked out through the dribbling windscreen at the pitch. It was bordered by backyard fences at either end, by the stand on the nearest side and by a bare white hill on the other. I could see straightaway that the pitch collected half the rain that fell on the hill. Hence the angry black mess down the centre of the field from one end to the other, like a huge trail of spilt gravy. It looked like a lot of things, but it didn't look like a lark.

The timber stand was an elaborate Victorian structure raking up to an improbable height for such an exposed location. Either side, thick rusty steel props had been set up to brace it. Boys in red were trooping out of the tunnel as we arrived. ''Ere we are: the Whinely Juniors,' Bob said. 'Warders' sons, half of 'em. Some real talent there. Whinely might make it to the top again one day.' He paused judiciously. 'Top of the Squeeze Cheeze League, that is.'

We went up and sat on a bench by the sideline. The stand creaked and groaned above us with every gust of wind. The coach was a big solid man with a red face and long trails of black hair plastered to his skull. He had a group of a dozen boys challenging in the air for high balls, in pairs. Half of those waiting for the next turn were already holding sore heads. 'Come on, for Christ's sake, lads,' the coach was shouting. 'Contest it will you? Contest it! You, Turner: do it again. And do it right. No — I want Turner again, with you Clegg.'

Even then I didn't recognise him. Only when the other boys stepped away smirking did I realise the slim boy standing there, very still, was Tom Turner, Kate's son. I could see now how slight he was, without his anorak on. The big black shirt hung off his shoulders as if off a coat-hanger. He was watching the coach with a blank face, while the tallest and heaviest of the group stepped up alongside him and began to jostle against his shoulder. The coach kicked the ball high but not long, so the boys had to dash forward to reach it in the air. Clegg simply stayed one step behind and used his weight to knock Tom to the ground when the ball arrived.

The coach walked over to where Tom lay. 'Are you an idiot, boy?' he demanded. Tom sat up but didn't stand, his long hair full of mud.

'Bastard,' Bob muttered beside me. 'Name's Tozer.'

'Well, are you?'

Tom just looked up at the red-faced coach for a second, his black fringe obscuring his eyes. 'No, Sir.'

'Then why can't you just do as I say? Do you want to

play or not?' The boy stared past him now, as if distracted. 'Then bloody get up and do it properly,' Tozer shouted, making Tom jump. 'Don't let him walk all over you. Don't be so bloody wet!'

'Knows how to get the best out of 'em, old Tozer, dun't he?' Bob said, watching Clegg run up and crush Tom again. 'He's a bullyin' bastard. He knows as well as the rest that Tom Turner's a bit soft. So what? I mean, it's not Bayern Munich, is it? Look at him, havin' another go.'

'I've a good mind to have a word with your father,' Tozer was saying, loud enough for all to hear.

A couple of boys snorted. 'You'll be lucky, Sir,' one called, inspiring general mirth. Tom was holding Tozer's look now, very still and sullen.

'Your mother, then. Who is it? She's paying good money for this.'

'Mrs Turner, Sir.'

'Will she be coming here today to pick you up?'

'No, Sir. We live in Soppstone, Sir. I take the bus.'

'Don't Sir me, lad. Just head the bloody ball. All right?' Tozer turned to go.

'Yes Sir,' Tom said sarcastically. Tozer looked back, hesitated, then turned back to the group and set them all off lapping the pitch.

'When's their next home game?' I asked Bob.

'Saturday. Why? I thought you were flying off.'

'Not before Saturday.'

I asked Bob to drop me off back in Soppstone to see the travel agents, but once his van was out of sight I went to the sports shop instead and bought a good football. Then I sat in a tea shop, with my foot on the ball under the table, doing a fair imitation of thinking until it was too late to go to the travel agents. It was getting dim as I came out and the headlights were flashing off the water on the road, but it seemed to have cleared overhead. I bounced the ball once on the pavement and set off uphill.

It wasn't hard to find my way to Kate's house — there was only one road. Near the top I left the road and skirted wide behind trees to climb the last stretch, so I wouldn't be seen from the house. The black car was there already, parked slightly askew by the front garden gate. I approached slowly from the blind side of the house and placed the ball in the back yard, just out of view from the kitchen window. Then I retreated to the ruins next door.

It wasn't long before Tom appeared and found the ball. He was dressed in woolly red pyjamas, with wellingtons on his feet as if he'd sensed there was something out there to find. He didn't touch the ball at first, just looked around and made little movements with his feet as if to kick, push or control it. I thought I could see his mouth moving. He was constrained in his movements, as if tied to a post, and his pyjamas made him look even thinner than usual, blowing against his skinny frame like washing on a line.

There was a fine mizzle drifting in, and Tom's long hair was already damp, hanging over his face. I could see him start to shake. I was cold myself, waiting for him to go inside. Before long, the inevitable cry went up: 'Tom? Tom! Are you in bed or not?'

Tom looked towards the back door, then turned back to the ball and just stood there staring at it, waiting. At the last moment he tapped the ball just far enough into the long grass to hide it, before Kate emerged at the door wearing an apron and an exasperated expression. 'Tom!' she said, asking something rather than telling him off. Tom turned a mock-pleading frown at her, coaxing a smile. But behind her appeared another head.

'You think it's a joke, do you?' the man demanded in a deep voice. It was the bloke I'd seen before and my heart sank, seeing him.

'Don't Vic,' Kate said. 'Come on, Tom, come in. You must be frozen.'

'Look at him: he's shaking,' Vic said. 'He's no clothes on! I told you: we should have this fucking door locked, so we know where he is.' He turned back to Tom, who hadn't moved. 'Come on. In.'

Tom just glared back at him, then spoke to Kate. 'I'll just be a minute.'

'Now,' Vic barked, but Tom stepped away. Vic looked back to Kate, but she just frowned at him.

'You're as bad as each other,' she said impatiently and looked back inside the house. She had car keys in her hand. 'I've my class to get to,' she said. 'I can't be late again, or I'll never get that flippin' certificate!' She paused at the door a second and held a forefinger up to Tom. 'One minute,' she said, and was gone.

'Don't know why you bother —' Vic started to say, but the door had already banged shut. Tom and Vic were left facing each other, a few metres apart. Tom's eyes were wide open between the strands of his wild black hair as he stood at the edge of the tall grass and waited.

Vic seemed to recover his composure a little then, straightening the sleeves of his trendy black jacket and checking his watch. He put his hands on his hips and looked the boy over. 'You know what you need, don't you?' he said. 'A bloody haircut, is what. Look at you. I suppose it's the height of fashion now, to look like a complete girl, is it?'

Tom just looked at him, his eyes narrowing. Neither turned when the sound of the car engine started up on the far side of the house. They stood there as the car drove off, staring each other out.

'Well, Mummy's gone and your minute's up,' Vic said. 'You know, I think tonight's the night, lad. You've a free barber here. Come on. What are you afraid of?' He took a step closer. Tom leapt back like a startled rabbit, and kicked at the long grass around him. Vic lowered his voice patiently, but his frustration still showed. 'What do you think you're playing at?'

Tom reacted at last, calling out 'Football!' Instantly furious, Vic ran at him, but he ducked to the right with surprising agility at just the right moment and Vic found himself on all fours, the knees of his jeans green and wet from the grass. Tom took two slow steps away, scared now.

'A haircut won't bloody kill you. Do what you're told for a change.'

Tom blinked, sneezed and took another step away. Then, summoning a deep voice from somewhere, he said with bizarre authority, 'No one will make me change. I'll only change when I want to change.'

'If you can't talk sense ...' Vic shrugged and made as if to turn back to the house, then sprang back and shot out an arm at Tom, grabbing his wrist. Tom cried out in fright and tried to pull away. Instead he pulled them both down into the wet grass. For a moment I couldn't see them, or hear anything over the wind through the stone. Then Vic stood, his face and trousers wet. He had Tom hard by the arm, and he led him back grimly to the house. 'Don't be bloody stupid!' he said. Tom kicked out wildly. Vic cursed and grabbed him with his free left hand, hard on the back of the boy's neck, bowing him. Still Tom kicked back viciously at Vic's legs as they both disappeared through the back door.

The light was fading. I hurried along the lane, into the deepening shadow of the tree on the corner. There I stayed, listening and waiting for an excuse to break the back door down. But no one cried out. I saw nothing and heard nothing more — just stood there watching the garden darken, then the house, as one light after another went out.

I was thinking of my dad, with his hand digging into my skinny shoulder, making a mess of my hair with blunt scissors. By then the cold had cut right through me, through everything I wore, through everything I'd put between myself and that place. I could only stare at the white ball glowing dimly there through the grass, in the shadow of the black house.

# VI

'I suppose you know your Aunty Alice is ill?'

Stan caught me like a sniper before I could get to the shelter of my door that Saturday morning. I hadn't seen much of him over the last couple of days. I wasn't exactly avoiding him, and he wasn't exactly avoiding me, but we both felt more awkward with each other. There was an admonition in everything he said, since I'd hinted that I might stay.

I stood by my front door and waited for him to cross the rest of the yard. His limp seemed worse than ever. 'You might have mentioned it,' I said. 'You don't look that bright yourself.'

'Never mind me, it's your aunt I'm on about. She'll be expecting you to call.'

'Has she asked me to?'

'She shouldn't have to ask. Bloody hell — I shouldn't have to ask, lad. It's the least you owe your own aunty.'

'I don't owe her anything.'

Stan looked at me. 'That's it, is it? Finished have you? Right, I'll do some work then.' He walked away, leaving me feeling like ... well, like someone who won't see his aunty.

Bob was late giving me a lift, so it was twenty minutes into the match by the time we got to Abattoir Park. It was a different scene from training: Tozer the coach was quiet and everyone else was shouting. Parents were prowling along the sideline in packs, abusing and cajoling their children as if demented. Most of them were men of that heavy breed, ex-players, but there were a couple of women too, no less vocal or vicious than the rest.

'Get in there!' one man kept yelling. He was overweight in a way that suggested lost muscle, with aggression at a loose end. 'What are you waitin' for? Get in!' His voice was deep and hoarse with the effort, his face red. He put his head down in disgust as we passed by, and shook a fag out. 'What a bloody joke!' he muttered. 'Bloody Hell Fire.'

The mud-splattered children looked nervously out to the adults gathered along the line and summoned what ill will they could, to appease us. Looking back over my collar towards the stand, I quickly scanned the parents in the first three rows for Kate or the bloke called Vic. They obviously weren't there. Bob had dragged along a bag of oranges for half-time and plonked it now amongst those crowding along the sideline.

I didn't recognise Tom at first, with his hair cut so

short. He was sitting on a brick and timber bench in the same red strip as the rest, with his long white neck exposed to the wind. Beside him was another boy in an identical Whinely shirt, with another bad haircut. They both looked cold.

Whinely were losing, but Tozer merely stood on the sideline, in mute contrast to his performance in training. The boys looked lost out on the pitch, working hard for their age in such conditions, but getting nowhere as a team. Just before half-time, Tozer shouted at a defender to come off. He gestured at the bench vaguely and the boy beside Tom went on. Tom sat unmoved, his face blank until the whistle blew again, for half-time. Then he joined the others, standing behind them and scratching his head, embarrassed to be still clean.

Bob dragged his bag of oranges over, offering them around. Tom stood near Bob and me while he peeled it, a little apart from his team-mates. He took the top half of the peel off bit by bit with his thumb, then ate the exposed flesh. The juice ran over his hands. Then he turned the peel inside out and ate the rest.

'That's how I used to eat them,' I said. Tom looked up, juice over his chin. 'Messy.'

'Aye.' It was a deep accent close-up, more like my father than that of a small boy. His eyes were the same deep brown.

'Going to play today?'

Tom dropped his head back and stared out at the empty pitch. 'Don't know,' he said. 'Depends on Mr Tozer.' He turned around nervously to see who could hear, and then I saw dark bruising under the skin, across his left cheek and neck, running under the hard line of shorn hair like rottenness.

I wanted to touch it. 'Hurt yourself?'

Tom flashed me a nervous glance, then turned and walked slowly back to the bench, pulling his collar up. Tozer gathered them around him in a circle and bent over intently. His face wasn't calm any more, it was a picture of restrained fury. 'Are you scared of the ball, or what?' he demanded. 'Win it! Win the ball for me.' Then he turned on the solid, round-faced boy he'd taken off, who was smeared from head to foot with black mud. 'That was shameful, William,' he said quietly. 'Letting that ball go. Shameful.'

Bob came back from the stand as William limped off to the showers. 'Do what you can for Turner,' I said. 'Get Tozer to put him on.'

'Eh? Why?'

'He needs a chance.'

Bob looked at me, shrugged and said 'Y' soft bugger.'

As he made to go, I grabbed his shoulder. 'Right wing,' I said, and pushed him on.

Tozer listened, nodding impatiently, and a startled Tom took to the field five minutes later. He pulled at his socks nervously, and seemed unsure where to stand. He had that last-choice substitute look, as if dragged suddenly out of a private reverie into a fast, chaotic world. But the whistle blew and he leapt into life straightaway, running about madly and dodging the other boys as he'd evaded Vic.

'He's quick, I'll give him that,' Bob said after a while. 'But he can't tackle to save his life. He's scared.'

'They all are. That's Tozer's doing.'

'Shuusshh, for God's sake. He'll hear. He put the boy on, didn't he?'

'But look at him, Bob. He knows where the ball's going. He's just had the confidence knocked out of him.' Bob was looking at me carefully. 'Do you know the boy, then?'

'No. No, I don't, but if you see someone play you do know them in a way, don't you? Watch him, now for instance.' Tom was walking in, catching his breath as a Whinely defender took the ball up field. 'He'll run wide now,' I said, a split second before Tom broke free of his marker with a delicate little feint and received the ball near the sideline, turning towards goal.

Bob laughed as Tom got quickly flattened, and he caught me smiling too. 'You like this, don't you?' he said. 'I had no idea you were so keen. Did you used to play?'

'Left it behind, didn't I?' I said, picking out an orange from Bob's bag. 'Left a lot behind,' I said, tearing at the orange with my thumb.

After the game I suggested giving Tom a lift home, since he took the bus. Bob seemed alarmed. 'You don't just go giving lifts to lads you hardly know, willy-nilly,' he said.

But Tom didn't put up much resistance. He looked exhausted and sat silently in the back of the van as we drove through town in heavy rain. There was a traffic jam at the Co-op lights. Tom poked his head out between us. 'Do you know my mum?' he asked, of no one in particular.

'Yes,' I said. Bob looked at me. 'Used to,' I added, and got the look again from Bob. Tom was drained of conversation with that, and fell back to gazing out at shop windows glowing in the gloomy light.

At the foot of the hill he leant forward again and called out, 'Stop 'ere!' Bob braked hard, and I grabbed Tom's arm to stop him flying backwards. He pulled his arm free. 'I'd best hop out,' he said. 'You can see road from the house, and Mum wouldn't like me cadging lifts.'

'Fair enough,' I said. 'You got a guernsey, any road.'

'Are you Australian?' Tom asked, half out the back door. 'Cool. My mum says we might go one day — to Australia. I want to, but I don't think we will, really.'

'Why not?' I asked, but he was already jumping out the back, bag in hand. He waved once, with the rain bouncing off his arm, and then he was gone past the first trees and into the mist of drizzle and bad light. 'Seems happy enough,' I said.

Bob turned the van and took the first road uphill towards Goodley. 'When we get back,' he said, 'perhaps you can tell me what this is all about.'

We stopped at the Throttled Hen on the high road between Goodley and Bonklow Moor. 'The bitter's special,' Bob said. Timber saloon doors had been installed inside the entry porch and the man behind the bar was wearing a stetson. There was the faint sound of Mrs Mills' honky tonk in the air too, which seemed deliberate. 'They've done a Theme,' Bob explained. 'But the bitter's still special.'

We took a table in the back corner, surrounded by dark timber panelling. Half the opposite wall had been taken out and a new timber and glass room added on beyond, with spectacular views across the valley of more miserable weather on its way. We tasted our Special and nibbled our complimentary Mucho Mecana Nachos. Roy Rogers burst into song somewhere. 'This is what I'll miss most in Australia,' I said, 'authentic English culture.'

Bob only grunted but that might have been the nachos. 'What's this business with young Tom Turner?' he said.

'Just helping.'

'Come on mate. Y' knew his mother, y' said?'

I took a long draught of bitter and wiped my lips. Bob just kept on looking at me and fiddling with his car keys as if weighing up whether to go. 'I knew her in Manchester, before I left,' I said. 'She was one of the crowd there. It was a scene, we all hung out. We were all in one band or another. You know.'

'No. No, I don't actually, George. I know about bein' on dole, an' doin' bugger all, because I've only oddies for bread and milk. I know about watchin' Neighbours twice a day.'

'You're a sad bastard, Bob Gallagher.'

'I am at that,' Bob agreed and drank with great satisfaction. 'So. She's an old flame, Kate Turner?'

'It's ancient history, Bob. She has a bloke, anyway.'

'And how do you know that, might I ask? And why give Tom a lift, if you're so uninterested?'

'Oh, because he tried hard at training, and he was getting cold standing there,' I said. Bob just raised a heavy eyebrow and waited. 'All right, because he could play, given a chance. He's just scared.'

Bob was still staring at me, waiting. I sank back wearily against the padded bench and sighed. I looked him in the eye. I saw a man I could trust. 'And because he's my son,' I said.

'Oh.'

'Yeah, oh.' I smiled painfully but Bob didn't smile back.

'This is all just drink, right?' he said. 'This is just the sort of rubbish blokes come out with once they've had too much.'

'If you say so.'

'Tom is your son?'

I nodded. 'I wasn't sure before, but today I could tell. I could see it.'

'You've no actual proof, in other words,' Bob said. Then he stared sternly at me and shook his head. 'No. No, he can't be. He plays too well to be yours.' We laughed, and he put his hand on my shoulder as if he'd known me all my life. 'Come on, mate: out with it. The whole match report. The full ninety minutes.'

I drew a map of wet lines on the table. 'There's no big story, Bob. We got together because we were both out of our heads, at first. Like kids do. It was one of those things, when you wake up next morning with someone you don't even know, you know? Except this time it was different.'

'So you went out, the two of you? You were an item?'

'I thought we were more than that. I didn't think I'd ever be sitting in a pub with a bloke, discussing it like it was all over years ago. She was different from the others from the start. Younger, for a start. Younger than me, anyway. Even her clothes, they had that look — you know, Bought By Mum.'

Bob nodded. 'What happened?'

'Happened? It got hard — that's what happened.' I finished my drink quickly and stared into the wet glass. 'Dad was going on about emigrating ever since I could remember. He wanted us to get on, he said. It was always like a pipe dream, you know? Well, maybe you do. Always talking about it with Mum, and going to talks and films, dragging us along and arguing. Australia House and all that. He hated his job, I guess: he was just a pissy little estate agent, really. No way up. So this goes on for years, and then all of a sudden its all on, and I'm twenty-one, and it's well, are you coming or not?'

'You said yes?'

'Not just like that, no. I'd met Kate. But I had this shit job with the Post Office, and I could see what was coming, even with Kate: the bloody mediocrity of it, y' know? I mean, Kate wasn't going to get me a different job, or a place at university, was she? Then there's this other choice, this other chance. Mum was just assuming

I was going, like Dad. They didn't even know how I felt, I never told them much. They thought it was family that was making me hesitate: leaving family, if you can believe it. That had to be easier than leaving the football, the band and all the friends I'd had for years. Yet mostly it was Kate, though I'd only known her for a while. I just couldn't imagine leaving her, right then.'

'Because she were expectin'?'

'I didn't know that then, did I? She never told me. Maybe she never got a chance to, I don't know. How was I supposed to know?'

I must have raised my voice, because Bob reared back, palms up. 'All right!' he said. 'I just assumed you'd have to know.'

'Well, I didn't. I mean, I knew she was expecting *something* — I could feel that — but not a kid. It was more like she was expecting something from me, like she knew what was going on in my head.'

'But didn't you tell her you were going?'

'Couldn't, could I? What should I have said? I'm thinking of buggering off, love; do you think I should? I mean, now I'd tell her, ask her, whatever. But then I was too young and too stupid to know what to do.'

'So you just flew off without her?'

'My parents made it sound like a holiday. I could come back later if I wanted, but they'd sort out the emigration stuff in the meantime. They'd sort out every bloody thing. All I had to do was pick up the ticket and fly.'

'So you flew?'

'I flew.'

It sounded so simple. I was on that bloody plane again, in my head, and there was nothing out the window. Nothing at all. Only Alice had come to the airport. Only she had cried. I waved my empty glass at Bob, who was watching me. 'Another?'

'So how did she get on?' he asked.

I just shrugged.

'What do you mean?' he insisted.

'I don't know.'

'You don't know? You didn't ask? You didn't call from Australia, or write or come back?'

'No, Bob. I didn't do any of those things.'

Bob threw himself back into the padded bench, looking around for a witness, then back at me with that same judicial air I'd grown so sick of in Stan. I stared back, widening my eyes in mock horror. 'Are you having another, or what?' He shook his head and I stumped off for my own. He was stuck in the same attitude when I got back. I tried to revive the debate about the Best Bond Girl, but Bob stayed mum. 'I'm sorry I told you, now.'

'So am I, George.'

'Look, I'm not the Yorkshire Ripper. It sounds worse ...' I faltered, with Bob's eyes on me. The beer was kicking in. My tongue was numb. 'I was coming back ... things happened.' I took a look at Bob's infuriated face, and at the Lone Ranger poster on the wall, but what I was thinking of was Mum in the hospital, so pale that last afternoon before she died. The sunlight flooding in through the windows, making her look worse than pale, like you could see right through her skin and there was no blood inside.

Bob shifted in his seat and asked pretty briskly, 'So who knows?'

'Me. You, now.'

'You should just go home. You're engaged.' It sounded tough, the way he said it.

'That simple, is it? What about you, then? Is it that simple for you? You've a daughter somewhere.'

Bob fixed me with a hard stare. 'No, I don't,' he said. 'So don't go on. I've no right to her. Nor have you to young Tom Turner. You can't go chargin' into people's lives years after the fact.'

I had no reply — I knew he was right — but I was seeing the bruising on Tom's neck again, the fingers digging into him, his skinny frame bent fit to crack. I was hearing the back door slam, and wondering at Kate, turning her back on it all. She'd seemed so hard, leaving like that to go to class. So unhappy. Could she have changed so much that she'd knowingly left them to it? Surely she'd seen the bruising. I had no rights, but surely Tom did ...

An empty glass was turning in its own wet circle on the table. I was holding it, but I couldn't remember drinking it.

'Come on,' Bob said. He was standing.

The saloon doors got me in the guts going out and a storm reared up before me in the carpark, grabbing at my jacket. The rain had paused, but the wind itself seemed wet. 'God, I'm cold,' I said.

Bob glanced down at me over the collar of his coat. 'No you're not,' he said, and he sounded angry. 'It takes years to get cold, George. You don't know what cold is. You've been away too long.'

I was leaning on his car. 'I don't know what to do now,' I said.

'Go home and sleep,' he said, opening his door. 'It's late.'

'No, no,' I shouted, as he got in. 'About Tom. I don't know what to do about Tom.'

The engine kicked in as I hit the passenger seat. Headlights leapt out into new rain. 'I said it's late,' Bob as repeated and the van lurched backwards. 'I said you should go home.'

There was a light on in the garage when Bob dropped me off. I found Stan throwing suds over the Cortina. 'Stan, why clean it? It rains every day.'

'Needs the polish.' He stopped and looked at me. 'Look, I don't need you to tell me how to care for Joyce's car, thanks very much. Thirty year we've had this.' He threw more suds over the boot. I watched them running down over the pristine curves of racing green. 'First car we ever had, this, and with a bit of work it'll be the last.'

'Dad wanted one, too,' I said. 'I remember he said: one day we'll have a car like Joyce 'n' Stan's.'

Stan smiled at my version of Dad's pompous baritone and he eased off with the sponge. He shook his head and scratched it, wetting his hair. Then he bent down and turned the sponge gently inside the rear lights, laying an icing of soap over the shiny chrome rim. I looked in through the rear window. The red leather upholstery was immaculate — the high back seats never used by man nor child.

Out in the yard I let the wind wet my face and wake me up on my way over to the cottage. I turned on the lights, but then went straight back outside, leaving the lights on and closing the door softly so as to not worry Stan. I was headed for the Pike, of course, and was soon climbing in gathering dark, letting the moon guide me south.

By the time I reached the ruined house I was getting horribly sober. All her lights were out and there was no car, and no signs of life in the garden. I squatted down in the lea of the tallest wall and listened to the wind overhead, feeling dizzy and much colder than before. Moonlight bounced off the smooth wet flagstones across the floor. I heard something nearby — a scratching sound. It made me feel watched.

There were droppings the size of bullets at my feet and clumps of torn grass in the far corner I hadn't noticed before. I looked out through the broken doorway, but it was just black. The sound came again, closer. I sat forward, with a smooth round stone in my hand and my weight on my toes. I thought of vagrants and criminals and ... well, beasts, vaguely. Then I saw something flicker at a small opening on the far wall. There was movement there: two moving points of light that looked like eyes. I stood suddenly and the eyes disappeared. Then I heard stones fall on the far side of the wall.

I ran at the only opening out of the room and into the lane. Turning, I found Tom facing me six feet away, frozen in a forward crouch as if about to run.

# VII

'I thought you were a fox,' I said.

Tom straightened, staring open-eyed at me, listening. He had his red anorak on, but underneath I could see pyjamas. His face grew indignant as the fright died. He shifted his feet impatiently. 'Don't be soft,' he said. 'There's no foxes round here.'

His voice so mesmerised me that I forgot to answer at first. High and incredulous, with random depths of tone, it was too strange, too familiar. 'I'm just checking out the property here,' I said, 'wondering if it could be restored — re-roofed and all that.' He was looking at me like a stray dog does, waiting for a word it understands. 'It's for sale, you know.' His face was so pale and smooth, and his brown eyes were so wide that nothing modulated his awareness: he was all eyes, all ears, waiting for me to tell the truth. My lies sounded hollow in the face of it.

'I've been watching you,' I heard myself say.

The hint of a smile appeared on Tom's face at last. 'I know,' he said. 'I've been watching you.' We faced each other for a second. I didn't know what to say.

'You gave us a lift.'

'That's right. Bob Gallagher and me.'

'Right.' He relaxed a bit, placing me, and looked into the ruined house. 'You wouldn't really buy this rubbish, would you?' he said.

'Why not? It just needs work.'

'Needs a bulldozer, is what it needs,' Tom said, as if reciting something. 'But the Council are obstructionist.'

'Who said that?'

'Vic.'

'Is that your dad?'

'No.'

'What is he, then?'

Tom's eyes glazed over. He blinked. 'I am not far from thinking that he is a shitbag,' he said, in a phoney French accent.

I laughed. 'He's what?'

'Estate agent,' he said in his normal voice. 'Reckons this hill'd be worth a fortune, if it weren't for the Council. He wants us to get out of here and move in with him. He's got a bungalow. Shit boxes, he calls these houses.'

'Maybe I should do this one up, then. Just to show him.'

Tom eyed me suspiciously. Then he leapt back the way he'd come, saying, 'Hang on!' He disappeared into the darkest section of the house, clattered about and re-emerged with the white football.

'This yours?' he said, holding it out at arm's length towards me.

'No,' I said. 'It's yours. So you can practise. You need to practise if you're going to get better.'

'What? You're givin' me it?' Tom shrugged and bounced the ball once at his feet. 'Good ball. Ta. But I'm not much chop.'

'You could be. Your coach — what's his name, Tosser — he's useless.'

'Mr Tozer. What do you know about it? Are you a coach or something?'

'I've seen you down at Whinely. I'm a talent scout from Australia. I'm on the look-out for young soccer talent.'

'Crap.'

'True.' I knocked the ball out of his hand, then flicked it over my head and tried to trap it on my back, like I'd seen on telly. But it came down way off target and hit my heel, flying back at Tom. He caught it. The whole thing looked deliberate. Almost.

Tom looked thoughtfully at me wobbling there, then stared off at the lights on the far side of the valley. 'So you're goin' back to Australia?'

'In a couple of weeks, yes.'

Tom wiped mud from the ball, glancing at me furtively. 'That's what I could do with,' he said. 'Professional help.' I smiled at this, but he seemed serious. 'You could coach me a bit, before you go,' he said.

'You should get your dad to —' I began, but stopped. 'You just need to keep trying. I've seen you play. You're all right.' He turned away. 'Look, I'd like to help, but —'

'Go on, then!' he urged, turning back on me with flashing brown eyes. 'Just till the next game. We could train, up here. It's just what I need. Go on.'

I looked back at the lit windows of his house. 'That'd be a bit weird, Tom, wouldn't it? Your mum wouldn't like it.'

'We could meet on t'other side of this, out of the road. Vic and Mum wouldn't even know.'

He held the ball to his chest, looking keen and hopeful. I had that sinking feeling, as if letting something happen without actually doing anything — something I'd regret later. 'You a goalie, then?' I said.

Tom looked cornered. 'No.'

'Then you shouldn't be touching that.'

Tom laughed and dropped the ball onto his foot. I hit it back on the full, hard past his face and into the ruins. 'You're right,' I said. 'You're not a goalie.'

He laughed and ran to get there first, so I chased him into the shadows of the broken home.

Alice, it proved, had only been in hospital briefly. She'd been there just long enough to visit her friend May, who stayed there whenever she could. Alice herself was as right as rain, she said. So we drove straight to Alice's Oldham bungalow, within a street or two of my old home. We could easily have taken a little detour and driven past for a look, but Stan didn't suggest it and I didn't ask. I saw the tattoo parlours and the off-licences and betting shops where clothes and groceries and books used to be sold, and I just didn't need to see any more.

Alice's bungalow was one street off the main road, in an old New Estate.

As Stan pulled up outside, my heart sank, seeing cars in the drive. 'This is a trap, isn't it?' I said.

'Just keep your hands where they can see 'em,' Stan said.

Alice was indeed well. In fact she blocked the passage, she was so well. She'd grown fatter than ever over the years, almost wedged now between the hallway walls as she wrapped me in her arms. I found myself tongue-tied, remembering our last parting at the airport years ago and a hundred Sunday teas before that, when Mum and I would go and 'leave Dad in peace.'

'How are y', love?' she asked, her voice huskier than I remembered, but otherwise absolutely It. My mother's. 'Have you had y' tea? We've a buffet on, so you can take y' pick.' Then she lowered her voice into grim chastisement: 'Evening, Stan.' Stan nodded ironically, and made to tip a hat he probably hadn't worn since 1963. 'How are you, you old goat?'

'Oh, middlin'. Be right, once I've had a drink.'

'Well, behave. Do you hear?' She raised a short finger in warning. Stan retreated, or advanced sideways to the kitchen rather, mumbling something mutinous. Alice turned on me again. 'Have a word later, shall we, young George?' she said.

As soon as Alice was settled in her armchair, her

husband Roy, as skinny as Alice was round, brought her a scotch and coke in a large glass tumbler. 'Well, Birthday Boy,' she said, 'I suppose we should make a fuss over you.' She was peering over her drink at Stan. It dawned on me that it was Stan's birthday.

Her voice had grown so hoarse over the years that I could hear her throat snap at the end of every word. She sat appraising Stan scathingly with a fag in her hand. She'd been the skinny one once — the cheeky, reckless one. Mum had been the beauty.

Stan made to retreat to the kitchen again, but Alice's daughter Denise blocked him from behind with a box wrapped in bright paper. 'Happy Birthday, Uncle Stan,' she said and kissed his crumpled cheek. He smiled, showing gaps in his teeth.

'Y' needn't have, love,' he said.

'It's from all of us,' she said. 'George too. Go on: open it.'

Trapped, Stan stood his ground and tore at the paper, finding evident satisfaction in boxed scotch wrapped in Y-fronts. Ribald calls to 'Try 'em on!' seemed to amuse him, and we were all soon treated to the sight of Stan pulling a huge pair of white underpants up over his trousers. This brought the house down and when Denise tugged another pair over his greasy grey hair, he only adjusted them slightly and grinned shyly at us, with his wild wiry eyebrows springing out from under the elastic waistband. Denise's dodgy boyfriend Noel joined in, miming a catwalk and it was absurd, and vaguely obscene, and such a relief from chatter that the room lost its reason.

All of which put Alice in singing mode, of course. The

men put the Y-fronts away and resumed indulgent poses as Alice rose at last from her throne and coughed in preparation, with Denise holding her waist from behind. 'We're missin' our Judith,' Alice said, and Stan hummed agreement. 'Eh, George? We're missin' y' mother, aren't we?'

Alice took a last awesome swig of her scotch, drew a deep breath and collapsed into breathy laughter, Denise cackling over it. Sobered by her own coughing, Alice quietened down, waved a short authoritative finger in the air and mother and daughter began, high and nasal, like divas with the flu:

> For we are the two Rochdale Mashers,
> and we often go out on a spree ...

Denise swayed behind Alice, with one hand on her shoulder and the other swinging free like Alice. But they soon had to stop, forgetting the next line and falling into laughter again. 'We're missin' our Judith,' Alice repeated. 'She were the only one that knew words.'

They carried on, but Alice's voice soon faded as some unspoken memory upset her. She had to hide behind Denise's back to wipe her eyes, swaying to the rough rhythm of her daughter's voice:

> And we dance
> and we sing,
> and we don't care a jot,
> we're a jolly fine lot.

We're all right
when we're tight,
and we're jolly good com-pa-ny.

Denise reached behind and pulled Alice's damp cheeks roughly to hers as they stopped and the family cheered. Then Alice dissolved into coughing again. It came in waves as she tried to tell a joke about the three siblings long ago, when they were all in the mill. She'd laugh and then bring on more coughing, and the story got nowhere. Roy stepped up with another drink and stroked her back. 'Will y' take it easy?' he said in warning. 'Will y' slow up, or do I have to put y' to bed?'

'No danger of over-excitement there!' Alice said sullenly, then dissolved into laughter again, red-faced and wobbling. This time she couldn't stop coughing and the whole room grew quiet, watching her and listening to her straining breath. Still she tried to speak, as if her life depended on raising a laugh, but the tension built as she struggled for air. Denise brought water and kneeled at Alice's feet as she drank.

When she finally settled and her shiny crimson face paled a little, Alice was melancholy. 'I always thought we'd all get together again, the three of us,' she said.

'Not to be, love,' Stan said gently. 'No use goin' on about it.'

'I'll be next,' Alice said, resting her chins on her little fist. 'There might be just Stan next time our George graces us with his presence.' Murmurings of protest and denial arose all around her, but she waved them down with elegant little gestures. 'It comes to us all,' she murmured back with music hall melancholy. 'It comes to us all.'

Roy surreptitiously took the remains of her scotch away. 'Y' sound just like y' mother,' he said. 'Dun't she?' he pleaded to the room at large.

'Aye,' Alice agreed, 'and where's she now?'

'Pushin' up daisies,' Stan said, smiling.

Noel took Denise off then, and I found myself facing Alice alone, while Stan and Roy talked football in the kitchen. 'What do you think you're doing, staying over at Stan's?' she demanded. 'I thought you had a fiancée to see to.'

'I'm on holiday.'

'What's this: separate honeymoons before wedlock? Have you heard this, Stan? He's on honeymoon on his lonesome.'

Stan stayed in the kitchen and just waved a tea towel at us behind his back.

'Don't Alice,' I said quietly.

'You sound terribly secretive all of a sudden, our George,' Alice said, eyes narrowing. 'How long have you been here, and never once over to see your aunty until Stan drags you over by the scruff of the neck.' Her eyes, besieged by flesh, were moist and blurred. 'What is it?' she asked very quietly. 'It's not Kate Turner?'

I stared back as blankly as I could. The conversation in the kitchen had dimmed, having caught our changed tone perhaps, if not the words. Alice sat back in her chair, watching me watching the kitchen door. 'You're a worry,' she said.

'I don't know what you're talking about. I'm just having a holiday. Or trying to.'

Alice shook her head slowly and struggled to rise. I had to get up and help her, holding her arm. 'Come on,' she ordered, gripping my wrist firmly. 'I've something for you.'

She led me through the hall to a spare bedroom at the back of the house. She sat me down firmly on the bed like a child and dragged over a large cardboard box from the wardrobe. One by one she pulled out objects wrapped in browning tissue paper and laid them out on the floral polyester eiderdown: a murky glass vase, a tin tea service with fake silver peeling off, old plates and cutlery, a photo album …

'We were to send these on,' Alice said. 'But with your mother going so quick after leavin', y' dad said not to bother. He had no use for 'em, he said.'

I handled the bowls and souvenir Blackpool spoons reluctantly. They were sad and cheap. I couldn't blame Dad for leaving them behind.

'It's all yours by rights, any road,' Alice went on, her customary authority deserting her now as she surveyed the mess on the bed. 'Do you not want anything, as a keepsake? How about this?' She opened the album and black and white photos spilled out over the eiderdown. I caught a glimpse of my parents on a scooter together, and another where they were standing on a pier. One of a soccer team lined up on a pitch with Dad in the middle of the front row. Captain Dad.

'No, Alice. I haven't room. I'm travelling light.'

Still Alice fiddled with the stuff, matching lids to pots. I shuffled the photographs back into the album, shut it, and put it back in the bottom of the box. 'It's not much, I know,' she admitted. 'I think we've sold the better things, if truth be told. They hadn't much anyway. That's why you all went, eh? Opportunities.'

'That right?' I piled things back into the box less carefully than before and Alice watched. 'Chuck it all out,' I said. 'It's just taking up space.'

Alice sat on the bed wearily and it sank heavily under her. 'Are you sorry you went, is that it?' she said gently.

I laughed, but it sounded bitter. 'It's too late to be sorry now,' I said and folded away a silver-plated cake stand I remembered all too well. I tossed it back in the box with the rest.

'You weren't to know about your mother, were you? Or is it Kate? I didn't think you were serious about Kate Turner.'

'It's nothing to do with Kate. I don't know why we're —' I pushed the box back into its hiding place, to calm myself. 'You can keep all this stuff,' I said and closed the wardrobe hard. 'It's no use to me.'

'If we'd known,' Alice began, 'that you and Kate were —'

'I'm on holiday,' I said, then lowered my voice. 'That's all.'

Alice still sat on the bed, looking at the wardrobe door. 'You have seen her, haven't you?' she said. 'I'm not stupid, George. I may not have been to bloody grammar school or have a scholarship or whatever it is you have, but that doesn't make me stupid. So don't talk to family as if they're children, and don't lie to us.' She took a deep breath and gave me a look that still sent a shiver down my spine after all those years. 'Now: have you spoken to Kate or not? Yes or no?'

'No.' This seemed to satisfy her, at last. 'N. O. No.'

'Well, that's all right, then, isn't it. There's no call to. I spoke to her after you left, you know that, don't you? I knew where she worked, at the hospital. I let her know about your mother. I tried to explain.'

'Oh, I'd love to have heard that, Alice. I'd love to have heard you explain it all to Kate.'

'I were just lettin' on, as to why y' wouldn't be coming back, that's all. She weren't right pleased, George, I admit, but she knew then about your mother passing away, at least. Knew your dad needed you over there.'

'Whatever. It's a bit late now.'

'Aye, well. Be as it may, I thought I should at least —'

'It amazes me, Alice, how much you think about other people's business.'

She pulled herself up at this, and let air out through her teeth. 'If that's meant to be rude, young man, you'd best go practise.'

'I'm sure Kate was ruder.'

'She wasn't like that, George. She was very civil to me, as a matter of fact. I'll give her that. I've always said she'll come to naught, and I've heard nothing since to prove me wrong, but she's always been civil. She's had a few men since you, you know. She didn't take long to get over you, you know, from what I hear.'

'I don't want to hear what you hear. Look, Alice: I don't want a row.' I got up to go, which sank her further into the bed.

'There's more than one knocks on that girl's door, even now.'

Turning back on her, I couldn't keep the anger out of my voice. 'That's not true. Just don't say that, Alice. You've no call to. You're wrong.'

Alice scrutinised my red face then. 'What would you know about it?' she asked quietly.

'I'm just not listening to gossip like that.'

Alice looked very hard and very shrewd indeed, and I remembered she was my mother's older sister, and a bossy one at that. 'Seems to me you're listening very well, our George,' she said.

'It's time I got back,' I said.

'It's time you got back to your fiancée, is what it is,' she said in a lighter tone, and I helped her up off the bed. She already regretted mentioning Kate, I could tell. Back with the others, she flooded me with questions about Vanessa and the wedding. They planned to visit Australia, she said. Maybe they'd make it to the wedding. I didn't believe it for a second. It was too late anyway, after ten years of leaving us to it. It was too late to divert me from Kate Turner as well.

# VIII

'Are you going to throw up?' Tom asked from a safe distance. He stood there perfectly composed, trying to irritate me with his slow, even breathing and his what's-next demeanour.

'No, I'm not going to do very much at all, for a minute.'

'You look shocking.'

'Look, just sit down for a minute, will you? You're ... you're probably more tired than you realise.' I patted a damp rock next to mine. With a glance towards the rough rectangle scratched on the wall as a goal, he reluctantly took a spot a little further off.

'Not tired,' he muttered mutinously. 'Anyway, when are we going to start training?'

'We have. This is it.'

'Yeah, but proper, like?'

'I thought we might just ... well, kick the ball about a bit, like we're doing.'

'What about SSD?'

'Well, you won't catch it playing football.'

'Sequential Skills Development. Aren't you going to teach me tricks and that, and positional ploys, and zonal defence and that?' His hands were on his hips, and puzzlement was rapidly budding into indignation.

I rubbed my chin a bit. 'Er, yeah. We could do that, Tom. No problem. STD, no problem.'

'SSD.'

'Right. Thing is, Tom: that's not really my particular area of expertise.'

Tom was looking at me as if he wanted his money back. 'What do you do then?'

'Well, say there's a player that's — well, let's say he lacks confidence — gets himself knocked about a bit, loses the ball rather than take a player on. Know the type?' Tom started nudging the ball softly against the opposite bank. 'Not because he can't beat him, but because its easier to get knocked over, in a way. Right? Know what I mean? Well … I'd sort that out.'

'How?'

'By helping him out instead of putting him down. By helping him to use that self-belief that every player has in him … somewhere.'

'How?'

'Well, by applying psychological profiles …'

'How?' he snapped.

'In specific ways …'

'How?' Then he just raised his eyebrows at me, in a scathing, world-weary way and smiled. It dawned on me that he was taking the piss.

The subject was dropped.

But Tom seemed more trusting, if anything, from then on — as if he had my measure. Which I guess he had. There couldn't have been much 'training' to it, even if I'd known what I was doing. I'd be gone in a few weeks anyway — I couldn't teach him much, beyond the rudiments of self-defence. I just wanted to help him beat the fear so he could really take it on — the game, and a few other things, too. Vic, for instance. He just had to stay on his feet.

By cutting into the dark crust of moss with a sharp rock, I had marked a goal on the north wall of the third house at the far end of the lane. The land dipped on that side to form a bit of a hollow, so we couldn't be easily seen there, and the ball didn't roll off the hill every five minutes. Tom was ridiculously keen, as if he'd never kicked a ball around before. Any awkwardness between us — the sense that we were doing something wrong — dissolved in a flurry of ball work. Tom's persistence surprised me; even if I accidentally tackled or kicked him too hard, he never made a sound, just set his teeth and came on for more. I started to see how Vic could dish out the odd thumping and Kate know nothing about it.

'Does Vic play with you, then?' I asked, late on that first day.

Tom shook his head, dismissing the question, and gestured for the ball. 'Would you want to play?' I asked. 'Professionally? There's traineeships, you know.'

'Couldn't.'

'Why?'

'Vic.'

'It's down to your mum, isn't it? Not him.' Tom just shrugged. 'What's he like, this Vic?' Tom shrugged again, staring at the floor. 'You're good at that,' I said. 'Champion Shrugger, Tom Turner.' He shrugged again but it was a joke this time. Not that he smiled. 'Do you like him?' I asked.

Shrug. But he had his eyes on me now.

'Hate him?'

Shrug.

'Does he eat people?'

Shrug. Then a frown. 'Eh? Does he what?'

'Is he an alien? Does he keep toast in his socks?'

Tom smiled despite himself, embarrassed on my behalf. 'You're barmy.'

'Yeah, I'm barmy and you're a zombie. You switch off, do you know that? Don't Tom, you can't afford to. Not now, and especially not on the field. Not at home either, for that matter. Keep an eye out for who's around — who's on your side, their side, where they are, whatever. You need to know. You need to be looking, thinking, listening, so you can control it. All right?'

He shrugged, but he didn't look carefree at all, he looked painfully vulnerable, with those narrow, bony shoulders poking out under his shirt. He looked like a bloody orphan, and for the hundredth time I wondered at Kate, that she should let it come to this. But then he laughed at me — I must have been the one that looked a zombie — and he was past me before I knew it, and scoring.

On the second day the wind was gusting violently, with rain coming and going like sea spray, so the ball had to stay down and our hoods had to stay up. I began to run at Tom and tackle him a bit, then show him what I'd done, how his light body pivoted easily over my shins if he just blundered in. Then I got him to try to pass me. Sometimes I'd let him past, other times I'd cut his stiff little legs out from under him as viciously as I dared, until he began to anticipate and try to fool me.

As afternoon turned into evening, we stood beside the lane waiting for Kate to call for him, and a rare stream of sunlight flew up the hillside like an exotic bird. 'Be cricket season soon,' Tom said with disgust.

'They play soccer all year in Australia, you know,' I said.

'Rubbish! You're joking!'

'Local leagues in winter, national league in summer. Plus English and European football on telly. It never stops.'

'Flippin' 'eck! Where do I sign? Mum says it's always sunny an' that over there. She's always on about Australia.' Tom looked at me as if expecting me to say something and kicked at the grass. 'But Vic reckons it's rubbish — Australia. Reckons they're all morons there, and there's nowt but kangaroos and sand.'

'You don't have to agree with Vic.'

'I don't,' Tom said, with quick defiance. He kicked at

the grass again. 'You're not really going back there, are you?' he asked suddenly, with an attempt at disbelief.

'Yes.'

'But why? You've only just got here, haven't you?'

'I'm getting married.'

'Yuck.'

I laughed. 'You might be right.'

Tom had me in his sights, focussing hard through narrowed eyes. 'What do you want to marry for? Mum hasn't. Is she dead gorgeous or something, your 'un? Why'd she want to marry you, if she's so gorgeous?'

'Cheeky beggar!' I thumped him gently in the ribs and he wriggled away, but he was still wanting an answer, I could see. 'Because her daddy's dead, if you must know,' I said. 'She loved her dear old daddy and she needs another one.'

'Eh?'

'Forget it.' I leant on what must once have been the kitchen hearth. Through the window openings on the far wall, I could see Kate's house. 'Is that your window?' I pointed.

'Don't be daft.'

'You always think I'm daft.'

'Don't be, then.'

'Eh!' I raised a finger in warning, echoes of Stan and Alice in my voice. 'Where is it, then? Does it face down the hill, or what?'

'Don't be daft. It's on t'other side, facing the trees. Why do y' want to know?'

'I'm just nosy. Is it a big room?'

'If you're a mouse,' he said. 'Look, say this is it, in here.' He waved around at the old kitchen. 'That's my window, right? And that's my bed.' He bounced the ball off the opposite corner where a large stone lintel lay flat.

I went and sat on the stone, boots in a pool of water. 'Mmmm, comfy,' I said. 'Got any posters?'

'Course! That's Ryan Giggs over there on that wall, and Cantona's on that'n, watching me back. He's a bit torn now. I used to have a couple of Liam Gallaghers from Vic's magazines, but I can't stand him now. He's gone soft.'

I lay down on the old lintel, squirmed luxuriously on the cold stone. 'Thanks for asking me over, anyway Eric,' I said, addressing the bare wall. 'Nice place you've got here.' Tom laughed out of generosity, looking down curiously at me. Then we heard Kate calling. I straightened up from the hard bed, full of words of wisdom and a defence of Liam Gallagher, but Tom just wasn't there any more.

It was exhausting, of course. I had to walk there and back as well as run about trying to keep up with him. Which was why I found myself sitting on a damp rock so often, offering talk instead of action.

'You'll be much better Saturday, after all this.'

As usual, he just stared back at me, as if waiting for something better. I'd got used to that. It was a look you might mistake for blank, if you didn't infuriate your fiancée with the same look yourself. He was hearing me all right — he just wasn't going to admit it. 'Just push forward, like I showed you — over the ball. Give them space to foul you, if they want to make it obvious and get a free kick that's fine, but always push the ball on. Play your own game.'

He looked far from convinced.

'You're dreading it, aren't you?' I said. 'Saturday?' He looked straight at me and nodded. 'Why?' He wouldn't answer. 'You should be looking forward to it.' He picked at the ball's stitching, which had taken a beating from the stone wall. 'I'll see you there, then, I guess.'

'Might not go,' he said.

'What?'

'Might give it a miss.'

'Well, Vic'll be very glad to hear it, I'm sure.' It sounded nasty, and Tom looked aggrieved straightaway. 'Look, Tom: don't do that, don't run. Go. Be there. If it worries you, face up to it. It does no good to run away.'

'I'm only talking about one week.'

'Except then it's even harder to go back the week after, isn't it?'

'Yeah.' He looked away. 'All right.'

There were flecks of dried mud on his forehead that I badly wanted to brush off. 'It's my last chance to watch, anyway,' I said.

'You're not really going back to Australia?'

'Don't change the subject.'

'Sick of the weather or somethin'?' He wrinkled his nose up at the cold air. 'It'll clear up soon. It'll be spring. There's flowers and that. Don't you like it around here?'

I just shook my head, thinking of another missed

94

spring. Snow was still sprinkled loosely over the crest of the opposite hill, icing sugar over a cake I could neither have nor eat. Tom's big brown eyes were puzzled. 'Oh, I like it enough,' I said at last. 'But that's a secret. Between you and me, mate, I like it a damn sight more than your mother's precious Australia. It's useless here really, I know, but I love it. I don't really want to go at all.'

'Then why are you?'

'That's where I live now. That's where Vanessa lives.'

'But you used to live here? Why d'ya go, then?'

'Maybe I ran away.'

'But you told me not to.'

'I was right, too. Don't. Don't end up like me. However hard it gets, stay where you belong.'

Tom pulled his collar up around his neck and stared back at the chimney of his house, which seemed to rise up out of the far field like a gravestone. 'I have been hurt too many times to ever believe that I belong,' he said, in that dumb French accent. I was reminded, while he struck this crazy pose, that it wasn't just football that Tom was afraid of. I forced myself back onto my feet and kicked the ball from under his foot.

I tipped Tom over, but broke his fall with my arm. 'If someone's bigger, be smarter,' I said, and wiped the mud from his ear. 'What's he going to do? Think — where's he going, where does he expect you to be? — and just don't be there. Be elsewhere, Tom, and take the ball with you.' I brushed flecks of mud from his brow. 'All right? Then you win.' I went on like this, spelling out rules one by one that I was planning to break myself.

Tom had training the following afternoon, so I worked with Stan all day moving sheep, as I had when I first arrived.

'Not feelin' the call o' nature today?' was all he asked, and all I had to do was shake my head in reply. He knew something was up but he was damned if he was going to listen to me lie about it. I saw him glancing up towards the Pike a moment later, as if trying to see what could possibly keep me there.

On Thursday Tom appeared right on time, but I could tell there was something different about him the moment I spotted him ambling up the lane. 'What's up?' I said. He just shrugged. 'How did training go yesterday? Where's the ball?'

Tom looked back towards the house uncertainly and shrugged again. But he looked far from indifferent, in fact he was furious.

'What's the matter Tom? If you've lost the ball, it's not the end of —'

'Vic's got it.'

'Why? Have you had a row?' Tom shut down entirely at this, not even bothering to shrug. Without the ball between us, it was tense again, and strange. Tom looked back at his house as if he might go straight back.

'Ready for the game Saturday?' No response. 'You are going? Did he stop you going yesterday?'

'No.'

Then we both heard it, carried by the wind — Vic's voice, a hoarse bellow like a foghorn. 'To — om!'

Tom instantly darted out of sight into the ruined kitchen. I had to follow, and we were both soon standing with our backs against the wall as if facing a firing squad.

'Tom?' called the voice. Then a pause, in which Tom and I exchanged silent conspiratorial looks. 'Tom! The weather, Tom, for Christ's sake!'

We stood there quietly for a while but Vic didn't call again. When we finally did move, something had changed between us — some pretence of normality had been dropped. I knelt down until my face was level with his. 'You should go back,' I said as gently as I dared.

He looked away. 'Not yet,' he said.

I half turned and leant my back against the wall. 'No hurry.' Over the top of the west wall I could see what had worried Vic: a heavy bulkhead of dark grey cloud filling the sky, rolling steadily our way.

He'd expected me to fix things, I could see, and now I was going. I wondered at myself, at how I'd let things come to this, with the poor boy expecting me to somehow make everything all right. I felt the distance shrinking between the storm and where we hid — the air compressing around us, compelling us to move — and it came to me that he was right in his expectations, though he hardly knew why. Perhaps I was the only one that could ever speak to Kate about it.

'It'll be all right, Tom,' I said, knowing I was only digging myself in deeper with every word. 'We'll sort it out. But you should go home now.' I put a hand on his shoulder, but he winced and pulled away as if I'd hurt him. 'What's the matter? Is it your shoulder?' He shook the question away with his head. 'Are you hurt? Has someone hurt you, Tom?'

'No.' Tom's eyes were very wide and very brown, and now that I'd finally got his attention they were trained on me in the picture of frank wonder and candour. So I knew he was lying.

'Tell me, if he has,' I insisted, but his brown eyes just went blank. 'Is it Vic? It is, isn't it? Look, you're going to have to talk to your mum about this.'

'About what?' He moved away. 'What are you on about?'

'Tell your mum, Tom. That's all you have to do. Tell her.'

'I — don't — know — what — you're — talking about!' he yelled skyward in exasperation.

'I can't believe she'd let this go on,' I persisted.

'Who?'

'Your mum. She should be looking out for you better.'

'Shut up!'

Tom turned on me and I saw real fury on his face for the first time, even as he moved away. 'Shut up about my mum! Who are you to have a go at my mum?'

'All right, Tom. Look, I'm sorry. I just thought —'

'Shut y' fuckin' face, all right?' he spat at me. 'Fuckin' talent scout!'

He was on his heels before he'd finished, around the wall and off. I watched as the wind caught him like an empty wrapper and swept him away. I wasn't quick enough or smart enough to catch him. I had no hold on him at all.

He stopped running halfway down the lane, and looked my way deliberately with a hurt and hunted expression. I waved an arm to say come back, not wanting to shout, but he just jumped the low yard wall and disappeared. 'It'll be all right,' I'd said, like a million parents at bedtime, but in truth I didn't have the foggiest notion if it would be anything of the kind. I only knew that if I didn't speak to Kate soon, I never would.

# IX

The rain set in then and it showed no signs of leaving over the following days. Between spells in the fields with Stan, I'd sit on my table and eat cheese alone, watching light streaming out behind spires and stacks on the other side of the valley before being swallowed by the rain again. I'd sit there in two jumpers and a scarf, waiting for God knows what, staring at the dead heater on the floor — cold as hell but too tired to care.

Despite the weather, that little stone box had lost none of its appeal. If only it had. It would have been easier for me, no doubt, if lukewarm baths and cold stone floors had started to pall. Part of me wanted that — wanted to miss sunshine and fresh fruit and Vanessa on the beach at dawn, but in truth I hardly missed them at all. Instead, I'd grown accustomed to those rooms as the days had gone by. Soft pools of light around the table and the bed now nestled companionably against bowl and book, the softness of each shadow a kind of warmth in the ever-present cold.

The rain lifted on Friday, and I headed off over the moor again. Tom didn't appear at the ruined house so I spent a freezing hour with my back against the damp north wall, stamping to keep my feet alive. The outline of the makeshift goal was already fading.

Tom didn't make it to Abattoir Park on Saturday either, so on Sunday night I stayed on at the ruined house until dusk and used the darkness to move under the tree, hoping to learn something from the kitchen window. What I saw was Kate coming and going from the stove and the phone, looking very tired and slow in an unflattering orange tracksuit that had seen better days. Only fleetingly, when she was talking on the phone, did I see the vitality and energy that had drawn me to her all those years ago.

Kate had shone for me then like a beacon, brimful of attitude and fight. She had been so young, there was all this hope physically visible in her, making her skin glow, making her shift endlessly in her seat at every gig as if permanently ready to go. And she looked like she knew exactly where she wanted to go, even if I never asked her. Had I cut off that route for both of us by leaving? Is that how Kate saw it? Did she think of me at all?

There was no great love affair to remember, after all — no romantic trips to Paris, or long days in bed with the world outside the window. Much of it seemed a drunken blur, in retrospect. It wasn't what we did together, so much as how she made it feel just by being there. Our one day in the country, for instance — just one afternoon in a field somewhere — had seemed so new, so well lit for a while, like a moment on stage because Kate was there. Warm grass stretched out above the river like a blanket, beeches and elms piled up into the blue on either side, and Kate's dirty laughter filled the air all the time. Sober laughter at that. Neither of us could believe it, finding ourselves there, free from the pubs and hangovers and half-furnished bedrooms that had become our whole lives.

We sat together and compared feet, if I remember right. The novelty of bare feet was too much. Kate laughed at mine, and I found her pale high arches ludicrous and irresistible at the same time. She had a sketchpad and she offered to draw my feet.

'Not my face, then?'

'Not if it's flattery you're after.'

I couldn't help thinking of how different it had been meeting Vanessa a year later in the carefully cultivated wilds of the university gardens. Maybe, like that place, Vanessa was something I acquired rather than inhabited, something I accumulated, along with the limestone, the accent and the vocabulary of Law. And the thing about possessions is, there comes a time when you don't want them so much. Every acquisition has a disposal down the line, it doesn't matter how much you want the thing at first, it stays out there, it doesn't change you, it just sits there shrinking every day. Then suddenly you don't want it any more.

Now, up on this windy hill, Vanessa had become

unreal to me, as unreal as everything else below, and along with this release came a building shame when I thought of her, a shame which I could not allow to turn to pity or love.

I leant under the tree at the corner of Kate's derelict yard, stamping my feet and rubbing my hands like an arthritic pensioner, and I watched Kate stir what had to be soup. She stirred it with too much care, as if afraid of it. She stirred it longer than you'd expect it to need heating and stared at it as if thinking, but she probably wasn't, because her eyes hardly moved and even now, surely, her eyes still lit up when she was thinking. She seemed more serious, more substantial. And miserable, maybe — just a wee bit thoroughly miserable all the time.

It didn't surprise me that she'd changed. It only surprised me that now, after so long, I still couldn't take my eyes off her. I watched her stir that soup and I forgot momentarily about Tom, who was probably in bed with a cold because of me. I watched Kate instead, thinking how little I knew her — where she worked, what classes she was taking that made her leave Tom alone with Vic. Maybe she just didn't care enough.

Yet this wouldn't wash, and I started to wonder about Tom, with his talent for lying and his instinct to defend and shield his mother. I heard again Kate's tenderness, speaking to him upstairs while I'd listened below. I felt the bond that had been between them then, and it bound me too, a tight band across my chest. 'You know he loves you,' she'd said of Vic, and I was relieved to find I still believed she meant it.

'No I don't.' Tom's reply sounded muted now, conciliatory even, compared with the cheek I'd had from him since. He hadn't wanted to fight with his mum, I saw now, and he was still a million miles from hurting her with the truth.

I left Kate to the long-hot soup and trudged off into the night, along what was now a familiar path. It was a path of retreat and it felt like it, yet increasingly it felt like there'd be no real turning back for me while Vic still slept under that roof.

I spent Monday much the way I'd spent the weekend — in the wind with Stan, moving sheep and repairing walls. The danger now was waterlogging as the higher fields thawed and the rain came on heavier. He wouldn't let the sheep out so half the lambs were trucked away that afternoon to larger farms below. Stan stared downhill to the paltry flock left sheltering in the old stables. 'Well, that's half last year's rates paid for,' he said.

We trod down the muddy path by the wall we'd repaired the week before. Stan grimaced every time he had to tug a boot out. 'All right, Stan?' I asked, but he just stopped grimacing.

The sheep begged for help once we were amongst them, and Stan seemed to sympathise. 'Might be the last lot, this one,' he said, and fondly scraped mud off his boot on the nearest woolly back. 'Can't see any bugger taking this place on when I'm gone.'

'Where are you going, Stan?'

'I'm not going no-bleedin'-where, but I can't see this being a farm twenty years on, is all I'm saying.'

Looking out through the unglazed windows at the rain brushing the hillsides in great leisurely sweeps, it was hard to argue. But when had it looked any brighter?

'You're still here, Stan.'

'Aye, and the field's still on t'other side, so we'd best get a move on.'

I'd almost grown to relish the work, however painful and slow it was, and however doubtful Stan's methodology. It stopped me from thinking, for a start, and it stopped Stan from drinking, which was even better.

I held no illusions about 'George the Farmer' — I knew as well as Stan how useless I was, how soft and ignorant, how ill suited to a 'life on the land'. There was no future in it anyway. The pleasure, as such, lay in the knowledge that it couldn't last. A few weeks at most and I'd be gone, and Stan would be at it on his own again, or more likely not at it at all. It was like student work on building sites and orchards in the summer holidays to me, a day by day proposition, with the future suspended.

Maybe it was the same for Stan in a way, after sixty years in town, knowing he couldn't keep it up for long. I don't suppose he ever lifted a stone that didn't feel like his first, all the time wondering if it would be his last. While he was working he hardly seemed to notice me. The work was simple and probably futile and our link was the same.

If we made rapid progress the wind would inevitably start to wail about us, whistling through all the gaps in the walls that real builders would never have left. Then we'd hear a muffled thump amongst the grass downhill and it would be a section of wall tumbling over, like the winter tide cutting into Leighton Beach. Sometimes stray sheep helped it down, sometimes just the wind, sometimes nothing more than time.

Stan would straighten his poor back and say ever so mildly, 'For crying out loud.' Then we'd clump back down to mend it.

Stan's complaints about the weather were as regular and predictable as the rain itself. They were vehement enough — the complaints and the rain — and Stan acted heartbroken every time the sky let him down, yet there was a formal quality to his complaint, it was as if form of court poetry or something. However heartfelt the cries of betrayal, I could see he never expected anything but rain. 'You like it really, don't you?' I said. 'Bad weather. You love it. What happens on a sunny day, Stan? Do you cry?'

He didn't get that, and he didn't like it either. He made to smack my ear, but that was just a formal gesture too.

'You're all the same, around here,' I said. 'I sometimes think that's the only reason Dad left. He was different. The rest was an excuse — opportunities and that. It was just the weather.'

'Just the weather — I like that.' With his sharpest eye Stan weighed first the stone in his hand, then me. 'How did he get on, over there, anyway, your dad?'

'I can't believe you don't know,' I said.

Stan just waited, like he could wait forever.

'Oh, not that well in the end, as far as I know,' I admitted. 'He thought it'd be easier, I think. Packed up all his cares and woe, and all that, and thought he'd get rich the easy way.'

'Always wanted it bloody easier, did Bill Fielden. He were that type. He were the same when y' mother were expecting you. Couldn't bloody believe it, he couldn't. Why me? and all that. Mind you, it were a serious business then. Nobody gives a toss now, but it were the end of the world then, if y' weren't married.'

I kept my mouth shut. I hadn't heard this before.

'That's why they were always on about Australia, Canada, Rhodesia … any-bloody-where. For a second chance.' I blew air out my nose, at this. 'It wasn't your mother's way,' Stan said. 'But y' mother never could cross that bugger. And anyway, you've done all right for y'selves.'

'No one's done all right, Stan.'

He went back to work even as I was speaking and when the rain set in he carried stubbornly on, not bothering to pull his hood over. His hair was soon flat, grey and glossy against his bone-white scalp as he suffered the rain without giving in to it, willingly taking on the inevitable without resignation or revolt. He could take it all on — all he could change and all he couldn't, too — and all I could do was try to keep up with the old bugger, stuffing-up good stonework in a washed-out field.

We ate together that night in exhausted silence, as

usual, and I left only when he turned on 'Melrose Place' full-bore. He was so deaf, I could still hear it out in the yard. Vanessa's favourite show.

She rang next day, as I was clearing the weeds behind Stan's house. She went straight to the point, as I'd expected she would. Which was precisely why I hadn't rung her.

'I've booked a flight,' she said.

'You're coming over? I was joking.'

'No. It's a flight to Perth, and it leaves Manchester airport at two o'clock Friday, your time. I don't want you to confirm it, or pay for it — yet. I just want you to be on it. But that's up to you.' There was a silence.

'Vanessa ...'

'Will you be on that flight, George? I need to know, because there's a refund today, but not tomorrow. It's too late tomorrow.' The tone was familiar — I'd heard her use it often enough on the phone to her work. I'd thought then that I'd hate to be her secretary. What was new was a current of uncertainty — fear almost — running like oscillation through her speech, so constant that I took it for distortion on the line at first. 'Well?'

She didn't trust me to return. Knowing she had good reason made me feel all the more ashamed and all the more determined not to show it.

'What's this all about, V?' I said.

'That's a stupid question, George.'

'Then I'd like a stupid answer.'

'So would I. I'd like lots of them actually, but I'd settle

for the main one: are you going to be on that plane?'

We both knew there'd be no wedding if I said anything but yes. Did she, could she really expect me to say no? It shocked me to see how it must look to her — how I must look.

'Yes.'

A pause. 'We'll talk then.' The phone went dead.

Three days. I didn't know what I had to do, but I knew it would take longer than three days.

I went back outside to the weeds, but they didn't look urgent any more, in fact they looked just fine. They lined the dark stone wall by the kitchen door, well out of the wind, and when the cloud thinned they grew a luminous green. In the spring they would cast a lime glow over that wall, maybe even produce slips of yellow or white, like little gloved conjurors. Between their tentative softness and the unyielding wall, there seemed to lurk possibilities I couldn't fathom — shadows or deeper light, it was hard to say, but I desperately wanted to be there to find out, come spring.

Stan was still working on the west court wall, but he stopped for a bit and watched me coming back. As I got close enough to speak, he took a look at the weed in my hand, bent down over his work and ignored me.

'What's this, Stan? What's its Latin name?'

'That?'

'Yeah, this. Bet it has some grand Latin name.'

'That? Oh aye, it has at that. Bognor Regis, that is.'

'What, like the town?'

'Aye. King of the Bog, it means.' He watched me for a

few seconds, then barked at me, trying to laugh.

'Very funny, Stan. Very bloody funny.'

'How would I know the bloody name for the thing? It's a bloody weed is what it is.'

'It's a tradition here, though, isn't it? I read about it: amateur Latin scholars working in the mills and the mines, working class botanists and geologists on Sunday field trips, all that. I bet you did Latin at school, didn't you?'

'Of course I did.'

'There you go.'

'That doesn't mean I remember a damn word of it, does it? Have you come all this way just to discuss Latin? Who was that calling?'

'Vanessa. You'll be glad to hear I'm leaving Friday.'

He stopped work then, and straightened himself without flinching. 'This'n?' he said, and I nodded. 'About bloody time,' he said.

'I thought I'd spend more time on this, though. There's the lower yard, too —'

'I managed long before you turned up, son, and I dare say I'll manage again.'

'Still, given the choice ... She said she'd bought a ticket for Friday, you see. Asked if I'd take it. I had to say I would.'

'George, if you say a thing like that, don't act like you still have a choice. You've made it. You made it a long time ago, if you ask me. One day — it might take a blow to the head, mind — but one day you'll see that.'

He sounded so sad, despite himself, that I kicked at

stones in the grass instead of looking at him. 'I'll be back to visit. It needn't be ten years.'

'Y'missus might have something to say about that, lad. There'll be no call for Her Ladyship traipsing about in the mud like us daft bastards.'

I laughed at the very thought of her out there. 'I don't like it when you smile, Stan,' I said. I don't suppose his teeth had ever met, exactly. Not like you might expect.

'Talk about dragging y' feet to the altar. What's y'problem, lad? Don't you want to be miserable like the rest of us?'

'Is that what Mum and Dad were: miserable?'

'I don't bloody know, do I? I must admit, mind, the rest of us were well short of over the moon when y' mum lighted on him. But who's to know, eh?'

'In other words, yes they were miserable. Was he such a terrible bastard, my dad? I thought maybe it was me, being difficult.'

'Y' father had a talent for making people difficult. If y' mother had been a bit more difficult we might all have been better off, if truth be told.'

'Might go for a walk,' I said, and he just nodded. When I crossed the road he was still watching, shaking his head ever so slightly like a lifeguard at dusk, watching a tourist swim out too far into the swell of the Indian Ocean.

As I climbed the hill, all the water in the world was heading down. I couldn't see it, but I felt it underfoot and in the lull of the wind I heard all around me the soft musical chuckle of water over stone, down all the little channels that ran under the grass. I skirted the top of the fields, and with a few days stonework behind me the energy that had gone into the grid of walls below sank in. Many were no more than a halting footprint in the grass now, the pattern as obscure as the purpose. A monumental effort had gone into this vast network of walls, reservoirs and diversions — an effort now prematurely ruined, mysterious before its time.

The familiar path to Tom's door seemed daunting this time, too. Something told me he wouldn't appear anyway — not today and not after today either. Did he have a choice? A jumping line of dark mounds lay before me under a narrow silver sky. Little trails of smoke drifted up from the foothills further south, rising to a bank of cloud that was like a blurred mirror of the hills. The clouds were coming down where the land climbed. You'd have to bang your head, it seemed, before you reached the thin mercury horizon closing like a door in the distance.

In Fremantle it would be different, I knew: the humid aftermath of summer would be blowing away. Fresh afternoon breezes and maybe showers at last, giving the lawns some respite. 'Three days,' I kept saying to myself, 'I'll be there in three days.' But no matter how sweet the thought of sunrise there, and no matter how cold my aching feet, the thought brought no joy, only the creeping sense of time overtaking me, panicking me, pushing me on to … what? What was I rushing back to?

By the time I cleared the rocky ridge and saw Tom's house below, encircled by spray, I hadn't the heart to go down and cower in the ruin again. Even if he showed, what could I say? To rouse the boy's hopes and then give him no help — how cruel was that? To say 'leave it to me' and do nothing. Yet what could I do?

I carried on across the watershed, so burdened with guilt and confusion that I felt like a criminal unjustly released. It was a muddy trough I trod now, favoured no doubt by sheep moving uphill after winter. The drizzle increased as I rose, as if I were surfacing into rain, and there was a heaviness to that building fall that promised days of the same, maybe years: a steady, seamless pall I remembered well, bespeaking a long wet thaw and a doubtful spring.

I reached the ridge above the house, where snow still lay, crystalline and moist now, dripping into grey grass. Looking down through the mist of drizzle I could still see the house, the high water mark of the sea of lives below. Kate wasn't here for the scenery, any more than Stan — this was just where people got pushed — here or the nineteenth floor, in Bob's case. They used to get pushed overseas, but those doors had closed. The country had turned in on itself, and still it pushed. It couldn't push Kate any further, so there she stayed, stuck in the mud of Soppstone.

Behind me, away from the house and the town, there seemed to be nothing — just a line of dissolution where grass melted into grey vapour. It looked a whole lot like nothing. Then the spray cleared momentarily, and I caught a glimpse of a bare plateau sloping gently away from me for miles, crossed by power lines, without a wall in sight. Rain spotted two brimming reservoirs of black water in the distance, and that was it.

The dark stone seemed to have seeped into the grasses at my feet, black coming out from under the melting snow. It wasn't spring flowers bursting through a winter crust, it was grim fact asserting itself against a chilling, beautiful lie. What I was doing there I could no longer say, but whatever had driven me out there had once brought Tom out too, out of the claustrophobic hold of stone walls to face the winter and find me.

I turned back to the house which was now only a faint grey outline against the mist. Three days. I only had to walk down that hill, knock on the front door and speak to Kate, and Tom would be safe, perhaps. It wouldn't take me five minutes, from where I stood. But how could I, without admitting what I'd been doing up here, spying on them, lurking in the dark with Tom like a pervert, breaking into their home?

And yet, the bald fact remained and would not be denied: I had to speak to Kate before I left on Friday, simple as that. I owed the boy that much. Not that Kate would thank me. Nothing would please her less, I knew, than seeing my face again.

# X

I'd felt more than a little trapped on that freezing hill without a car, without the freedom I'd always taken for granted in Australia to come and go as I liked. Now it was different. With the snow gone Stan let me borrow the Cortina so I could collect Vanessa's plane ticket, but I almost wished the snow back, in spades. I wanted a wall of snow at the door of my little millstone box — a wall of snow against every crumbling, dissolving boundary of Stan's little refuge. I wanted a blizzard from the west and gales coming in waves, crashing in from the Atlantic until we had to ram the bolts across the door and sit it out for weeks. I wanted the phone lines down — no voices from the other side of the earth buzzing in my ear, least of all Vanessa's.

But then I thought of the house on the other side of the moor, cut off from the rest of the world — dark figures in a dark house, closed in together, and I shuddered as if I still stood outside watching. There'd be nowhere to hide in a house of that size. You'd lose the heat in a minute if you didn't keep all the doors shut tight and bolted.

It was no small thing to drive down to Soppstone in such weather. There was still ice on the road, which meant the long way down, not risking the combe but crossing over the moor past the Throttled Hen, then around to the south and back to Soppstone in a great long loop. The black ice on the lane and the car's stiff steering were bad enough, without Stan's voice in my head, prophesying doom: 'You'll never get down in one piece, lad. They'll be scraping you off the canal wall, down by Rutley. I can't have the car damaged, lad, so take care. Joyce would never forgive me, if you rolled it. You have to know what you're doing, down that hill. I learnt that in the Austin.'

An image of the mangled sedan behind the barn pursued me as I drove out of the yard that morning, and flashed at every twist in the walled lane. Coming out from under the net of bare black branches at the intersection, I didn't feel like I was out for the day; I felt like I was leaving for good, after years marooned up there. The strength of the feeling surprised me.

The dark, pock-marked face of the hill on my left retreated, the sharp tip of the Pike dipping out of sight, then the land sped up and flattened out, giving way further south to a broad flat mass of grey roof and vapour stretching all the way to Manchester and beyond. As a kid I'd seen that dirty view often enough after Sunday School, scraping my best shoes on the mossy coping stones of the old church walls. Dozens of mill stacks had risen like periscopes out of the vapour then. Today there was only the perfectly bland grey pool and I circled it gingerly now, looking out for black ice.

The rain was down my back before I got halfway across the carpark. It made the sky as heavy and dark as an old slate roof, and like the slate and stone all around Soppstone town, it wasn't going anywhere that day. Down on Guard Street the buildings themselves would take flight before the rain lifted, it seemed, and I couldn't help but think of Australian clouds — vivid, sailing things that thundered and fled in minutes, leaving trees to drip dry in the sun. Here it was different: things stayed wet.

Coming out of the travel agency with a ticket in my inside pocket, I made my way down the Manchester Road, amazed at the dogged persistence of the women lugging bags down that street in the rain. The older ones had their hair scarfed tight against the wind, the younger were fully hooded and drawn, bright sports coats ballooning behind as if for buoyancy. As I say, they amazed me. I was all set to let the bloody wind have its way and blow me away once and for all. I had Perth's blue skies in my head, knowing I'd be gone in two days time, drinking cappuccino again and nothing but bitter about it, because I was doing it all wrong again, running away.

I'd settled into a perverse, silent rage at all this by the

time I got back near the carpark, deciding as firmly as I could that the whole place could go to Hell, and no doubt would whether I left in two days or not. Then, amidst the Astras and Corollas I spotted the distinctive black and chrome tail of the Zephyr steaming to a halt at the zebra crossing up ahead. Irresistibly, I stepped up pace to get near before the lights changed, and watched it turn left opposite the Co-op.

Hurrying along the unsheltered face of shops on Manchester Road, I swerved around a couple of women in their sixties (or possibly their thirties) having a leisurely chat in the rain. When I rounded the corner the Zephyr was parked one street down, outside a red brick Victorian building that had to be a school. Crossing its carpark was a small woman under a bright yellow umbrella, skimming the liquid face of the asphalt with the unmistakable strut of Kate.

I remembered that walk well from trying to keep up without skipping years before. Which had felt silly, being taller. It was the walk of a woman who wanted to get there and suffered the ground beneath her feet for that one reason alone.

I followed those determined steps slowly, with no intention of quite catching up. The sign over the entrance indicated that the school was now an Adult Advancement Centre, which accounted for a playground full of cars. I slowed halfway across it, making sure Kate disappeared inside, and took a few steps more. Then I stood there for a minute, in a puddle, knowing I couldn't go in, but reluctant to turn tail yet. I knew what the place looked like now, at least — the place Kate spent so much time at while Tom was getting his head smacked back home. I could take that bitter image with me, at least.

But I didn't get to walk away because the glass doors swung back open as I stood there dripping, and Kate stepped out again, opening her umbrella just three yards away and staring straight at me.

I raised a hand in feeble salute.

She stared at me doing that for no more than a couple of seconds, then she stepped down quickly and walked right past me towards her car. 'Forgot my bag,' she said, as if to herself.

'Kate.'

She looked back without stopping, and I said her name again, more quietly. She stopped and stared at me, stubbornly still and silent, ignoring the rain. She waited long enough to know I had nothing else coming, then walked on to the Zephyr, parting the puddles either side with angry black boots.

I followed on slowly, expecting, almost wanting her to drive away, but she folded her umbrella instead and sat in Vic's car, closing the door. When I came alongside, she wound the window down a little less than halfway.

'Hello, Kate.'

'What are you doing here?' She really looked at me then, and I'd never been looked at like that before. She couldn't say anything worse than what that look said.

'I'm back for a bit,' I said. 'I thought I might do a course.' She put her key in the ignition and stared at it.

'Listen, Kate: can we have a chat, or tea or something? Don't just run off, since we've run into each other.'

She laughed at that, took a deep breath and blew it out. 'I can't believe you just said that. Don't run away, let's have a cup of tea. I can't believe that.' She was talking to the dash and I was bowed over, dripping, trying to hear over the rain, not knowing what to say. Nothing was right, though God knows I'd expected no better. 'I can't believe this,' she said. 'I cannot fucking believe it. What are you doing here?'

'Told you. Doing a course. Short course.'

'I don't fucking care what you're doing, George. I just can't believe you're here.'

'Right.' The swearing shocked me. I didn't like it. Didn't like her, suddenly. She'd grown coarse. That's what Alice had called her: coarse. 'What are you studying?'

'Why? Why ask that? Who are you to ask anything? What am I sitting here for, answering questions from you? Have you any idea how many questions —' She broke off, too angry to speak.

'Look, I'm sorry Kate, but since I'm back and all, well, can't we have a drink? Can't we talk?'

'No, we damn well can't. Not for your satisfaction. Why the hell should I?'

'I don't know. Did you … I mean, have you got —'

'Don't you dare ask anything about it, all right?' She started the engine, but I could tell she was torn. It wasn't enough to go now, for either of us, no matter how awful it was to stay.

'I just thought we might talk. If we met.'

She glanced at me suspiciously then. 'I can't bear to look at you, George, never mind talk.' She jabbed the steering wheel with the heel of her hand in a short, measured gesture, her mouth set hard. Her face was red and swollen and had lost some of the shape I'd loved at chin and cheek. There wasn't an ounce of kindness in her eyes, just anger and hurt and a new confusion that scared me more than anything. She looked lost momentarily, and yet up for a fight more than she'd ever been. She took a deep, steadying breath, both hands on the wheel, and muttered something I couldn't catch over the engine and the rain.

'Pardon?'

She turned her face up to me sharply, too close. 'I trusted you,' she said and I stared back, numb, into the raw depth of her eyes. It was an accusation, not a confidence, and the memory of her came back now full-on. I felt my knees going, my head spin. There wasn't a damn thing I could say. 'Don't do a course here, George.'

'No. All right.'

'Don't be here at all, George. Just fuck off back to wherever, all right?'

'All right.'

'Stand over there.'

'Eh?'

'Go and stand over there. Go on.' She pointed ahead, towards the street, and I obliged, walking on a few dazed paces. Then she let the brake go and gunned the car straight at me, scowling through the open window as

I jumped aside. Ten yards off, the brake lights flashed briefly, then she slid into the current of cars trailing along Manchester Road, heading home.

That was the lesson for today, then.

The next morning, when it came, was Thursday morning, and the plane ticket said Friday, and there was just no getting away from that. It was also a week since I'd seen Tom, and I wasn't going to see him again by skulking next door all day. More was required of me if I was to see him before I left. I could do nothing for him — Kate had made that clear — but I could at least say goodbye.

Stan lent me the car with no questions asked this time: maybe because the rain had lifted, maybe just because I looked too miserable to tease. By eight that morning I was turning into the road below Kate's house, where Bob and I had dropped Tom off after training what seemed like months before.

Parking further down the road, I walked back, straddled the low stone wall and set off up the hill, ankle-deep in mud. When the roof of the house popped up, I switched over to the far side of the southern wall, crouching in the shadow of the beeches there. The house was to my north for the first time, which meant Tom's bedroom window faced my way.

With a lurch in the heart, I saw the Zephyr parked in the drive, and tossed up in my mind which was worse — a knock on the door, which meant maybe a call to the police from Kate; a thump in the head from Vic; or just leaving and never seeing the boy again. It wasn't a happy choice and I might have grown old making it if Kate hadn't appeared right there and then at the front door, making me duck so violently I put my neck out.

Between loose stones in the wall I watched her carry bags to the Zephyr, climb in and turn the motor over. She'd slid away down the muddy lane before I could even pretend to consider speaking to her.

Once she was gone I stood, knowing that even if Vic were home, he wouldn't know me. I heard a noise overhead then — the sash in Tom's window rattling, and I looked up to see Tom's pale little face popping out between white curtains like a puppet. He didn't look surprised to see me, he just grinned comically and coughed. Then he put his finger to his lips. So Vic was home.

His face disappeared almost immediately, and I had to watch the curtains sucked out and thrown against the wet stone wall, wondering if he would reappear. Then he popped up again and threw something out, before pulling the curtains in and closing the window.

A small white paper dart sailed out across the yard towards me. A paper aeroplane, spiralling now into the mud a few paces away. I picked it up and unfolded it. Written inside in appalling handwriting was

Si tu n'es pas spontané,
tu ne peux pas réussir

Relying on my schoolboy French, I got

> If you're not a bridge,
> you can't be a shed.

which made just about as much sense as his damned quotes ever did. The real message had been on his face. He was pleased to see me.

The curtains stayed drawn and motionless at his window. I folded the paper carefully and slid it in my pocket, then leapt the wall and ran around to the back door — running less to avoid discovery, more to outrun my own fears, which caught up with me as soon as I grasped the cast-iron doorknob of the scullery door. I felt it turn and I let it swing me in, as if it weren't my choice.

It seemed an age since I'd last stepped in there. It was worse this time, knowing Vic was inside — I wasn't facing humiliation now, I was facing a fist in the face and a boot on my neck, or worse. I knew men like Vic well enough and I'd never come off best with them in my whole life, law degree or not. Those guys always got you, because they were happy to fuck up their own lives entirely, and everyone else's too, if that's what it took to hurt you.

Like the recurrence of a bad dream, I found myself inside that house again, a house whose door I'd never knocked upon, whose threshold I'd never been invited to cross, skulking like the coward and liar I was in the scullery with filthy boots, drawn irrationally towards what scared me most — not Vic, but discovery itself.

It was very quiet inside. I could tell even before opening the door to the hall that Vic wasn't up and about. Afraid of the stairs nonetheless, I moved irrationally towards the lounge and saw pictures of Tom there — as a baby, as a toddler, as a boy on his first day at school. Watercolours, too, hung near the door, in a style I recognised as Kate's. They looked faded now, and juvenile.

Nothing else in the room looked familiar: a sofa with dark velvet thrown over, a woodgrain television, a tired paisley rug. The suspicion hung in the air of a rented house, furnished cheaply by others who'd never have to call it home. Every item spoke of the gulf that had grown between myself and Kate — of how little, perhaps, we had in common in the first place. Every excuse I could muster for coming back to England, for messing about with Tom, for standing in that house now, in risk of arrest — every reason I might have given for this sounded in my ears, and it sounded hollow. I was a stranger, an intruder, at best a mistake from the past. I should simply go away, and never return.

And yet the simple thought of Tom upstairs, the simple image of a sheet of white paper flying to me — this seemed to contradict and overpower every sensible thought in my head. I was on the stairs already, taking one carpeted step at a time.

It wasn't a new carpet, or a nice one — it was one of those old floral numbers that Vanessa said looked like vomit — but it kept my steps silent, and it brought me safely to the dim landing. Four identical doors faced me. If I'd belonged there, I'd have known which one to choose, but then if I'd belonged there, there'd have been no need to say goodbye at all.

I couldn't call Tom, I had to guess. Vic was probably behind one of them and probably — only probably — asleep. I stepped past the first two doors and faced the one that I thought would be nearest the south window.

The closed door stared blankly back, tempting me to run away. There was something forbidding about the neat, tight fit between stile and jamb. I turned the dull brass knob without a sound and let the door swing one, two, three inches clear of the frame. The faint light from the hall fell on the carpet in a pale line, petering out a foot into the room.

I thought I heard breathing. A small charge travelled the length of my spine. My scalp tingled. I was the boy now, afraid in his own home, braving the darkness alone. Afraid to speak.

The breathing stopped as I pushed the door wider. I saw curtains leaking light and heard a bed spring. Recognising the curtains, I stepped into the dark and closed the door behind me with care. Slowly my eyes adjusted to the darkness. The curtains glowed. I saw pale rectangles on the walls, a bed below the window. Two white eyes staring at me.

I knew by then that it was Tom, but neither of us spoke a word, both caught in a spell of fear that had entered the room with me. It was the atmosphere of a crime scene I'd brought, and I was the criminal. My selfishness seemed obvious suddenly, facing those eyes. I was there to make myself feel better — I couldn't do a damn thing for Tom by breaking in, and he knew it. His eyes moved from me to the door and back again. I thought what it might mean to Tom if I were caught there. He was just waiting for Vic to rush in, and it was no childish fear. Or if it was, it was mine as well.

'Tom?'

'Yeah.' He caught the conspiratorial tone immediately, adding a touch of awe. 'What y' doin'?'

'I've come to admire your posters. What are you doing in the dark?'

'Dunno.'

'Why aren't you up? Why aren't you at school?'

'I'm sick, aren't I? Mum said I could stay home, if I were poorly.'

'Are you?'

'No.' He sat up in bed, and I could see his teeth. He was smiling.

'Open the curtains, Tom. Let the bloody day in.'

'All right.' Suddenly sprightly, he leapt to his feet, balancing on the bedhead to tug the curtains apart. 'Hello, bloody day.'

The room looked bleaker in the light, if anything: colder, with bare cream walls. Besides the bed, there was only a wardrobe. On the walls Cantona and Giggs, where he'd said they'd be. Hanging from the central light fitting, a little plastic model of a plane, unpainted. Familiar, except it was an F15, not the Spitfire I'd once had. Everything about the room was eerily familiar, as if I'd been there before.

I crouched down on my toes by the door, across the room from Tom. 'Where's Vic?'

'Fast asleep, probably. Snoring his head off. Did y'

hear him, in the hall? He does this.' Tom sat down violently on the edge of the bed and crouched forward. He scrunched up his nose and gave off little loud snorts.

'Shuusshh.' I knelt down, finger to my lips, trying not to laugh. 'Shuusshh, you little beggar, or you'll have Vic in here.' His face went pale and blank when I said this. 'I've been looking for you all week,' I said. 'Out there.'

He shrugged, and picked up a little red book. 'Not allowed,' he said.

'Why not?'

''Cause I'm cheeky. 'Cause Vic says I'm cheeky, just because I stand up to him, like you told me to. He doesn't even live here, proper. He sleeps here and that, and bloody snorts like a pig —'

'All right, Tom. Shuusshh. You'll wake him. What have you said? Have you been arguing? I didn't mean to start you fighting. He's not a bloke to argue with, Tom.'

'I'm not scared of him, the pig.'

'Have you talked to your mum?'

'She's always on about money and rubbishing my school and saying one day and you deserve better and all that. I don't know what she's on about.' He snorted again. 'Vic's a bloody pig,' he said.

'You like saying that, don't you?'

'I love saying it.' He thrust his head out, eyes wide in mock ecstasy.

'Just as well I'm going, by the sound of it,' I said. 'I've just got you into trouble.'

'Going? When are you going?'

'Tomorrow. I've been wanting to say goodbye.'

Tom stared at me, then started leafing through the little red book. He found a page and read, 'I say to myself, I'm just passing through.'

'Who says?'

Tom nodded at the wall behind me, and I looked back to see Eric Cantona staring back regally, arms crossed like an emperor. 'Is that who you're always quoting?'

Tom nodded big exaggerated nods. 'He's my Philosophical Mentor.' Seeing me frown, he shrugged. 'They said that in 'Bang It In'. Hey, they warned us at school the other day about blokes like you. They said to tell our mum. She'll be back in a minute, y'know. She's only gone to the shop.'

'I'm not like that, Tom. I'm —' The words choked in my throat. There was just no way I could, or should, tell him who I was. 'I'm off,' I said. 'That's what I am. I won't be hanging around, so you needn't worry. When's your birthday?'

'April fifth.'

'Here.' I folded a fifty-pound note four times and tossed it to him. 'Early birthday present.'

I was half-expecting him to throw it back, like they probably told him to do at school, but it vanished under his bed in a second and he looked excited. 'Cool,' he said. 'Happy Birthday to you too, mate, with knobs on.'

I stood up, looking at him in his lousy blue t-shirt, wanting to go over to him, but knowing I never could. I'd done all I could for him, bar be the father he deserved. 'Listen, Tom: talk to your mum. Never mind anyone else — if anything's the matter she's the one, all right? I mean it. And be good,' I added. 'And I mean: be good.'

'Yes, Grandad.'

I narrowed my eyes and he widened his mockingly. I opened the door and his face grew serious. 'Eyes on the ball,' I said lightly, and forced myself to turn away and walk out, straight past the snorting pig and down into the cold.

I went back the way I'd come. Tom's window was open just a fraction. As I passed, a little white hand appeared again and threw another paper dart, before pulling the sash closed.

The wind had been building while Tom and I had traded insults upstairs, and it caught the flimsy paper plane this time and swept it down the hill. I watched it float on and on, heading for the trees at the bottom of the field. I had to run like a fool to keep the damn thing in sight, but I couldn't move fast enough in the mud, with fallen branches in the way, and I lost it amongst the trees down near the road.

Coming down to the lower wall, I was in full sight of the entrance to the drive, but I scrambled about in the undergrowth under the trees for a good fifteen minutes anyway. There was thick cloud moving in from the south with a blurred underbelly of grey, but I had to find the plane.

Finally, close to giving up, I spotted its sharp tail in a high branch of a beech tree over my head. I jumped, got a good grip on the rough bark of the lowest limb, and hauled myself up to straddle it. From there I reached the next, thinner branch and got my bum on that, legs astride. Steadying myself on the trunk, I reached up hurriedly and grabbed the plane, crushing it.

That's when I heard the Zephyr.

I hugged the bark, keeping very still, feeling the branch dip and twist under me in the wind as the muddy black sedan turned into the lane not ten yards away. I caught a glimpse of Kate hunched intently over the wheel, looking neither left nor right. Worried about getting bogged down in the mud, maybe.

As the car retreated, I sat up with my back to the trunk and unfolded the piece of paper. I read 'Un artiste, à mes yeux —,' but realised it was in French and gave up. Cantona again. I sat there in the tree like an escapee, holding a message I couldn't read and watching one last time as Kate came home.

# XI

Stan insisted on seeing me off. He didn't insist on driving me to the airport, mind — not even to the bus stop — but he did want to see me off the property.

He stood under his porch, as he had when I'd first arrived, but he looked a damn sight better now. Something to do with drinking one scotch instead of ten every night, maybe.

'You'll be needing these,' he said, holding out the oversized wellingtons I'd been using. 'To get you down the hill.'

'You don't want them, then?'

"Course I bloody do. You can post them.'

'Post them?' It was raining, for a change, and bitterly cold. I changed into the boots, put my shoes in a bag and stepped out into the rain. I looked at Stan quickly, verified there was absolutely no question of a hug, and took another step away.

'Eh! There's always a bed here, if y'must,' he said, challenging me to deny it.

'Right. Thanks, Stan. I'll come and give you a hand, eh?'

'Oh yes, I'll be lost without your bloody expertise, won't I?' There was a small cut on his chin from shaving, and it was bleeding. He dabbed at it, annoyed or upset about something.

'Will you miss me?'

'Will I ever, y'daft bugger. I'm just glad to see you off alive, son. You look like you're ailing. That'd be love sickness, would it?'

'That'd be right, Stan.'

'Well, I want pictures of the wedding, and our Alice'll want 'em too.'

'Come over. I've told you: I'm happy to pay. It's Dad's money. It's no skin off my nose.'

'Aye, well. It's a bloody long way, in't it?' He dabbed at his chin and looked at the red spot on his hand.

'Will you tell Bob I've gone? I couldn't get him on the phone.'

He nodded and scowled again as I picked up my bags and walked. 'Love to the missus,' he called as I reached the road, and I heard his cracked laughter for the last time through the trees. At the intersection I took a last look at the black Pike, the very picture of immobility against the fluid sky, and I thought what a waste of time it had all been.

Down in the combe the Tops were soon lost in a tangle of black branches and try as I might I couldn't see past.

It got warmer as I descended, and soon I heard traffic and smelt things I'd forgotten — oil, rubbish, maybe something worse. There was music too, with no visible source — canned anonymous music I knew I'd never be free of again.

When I rounded the loop over the canal I changed my boots again and slung Stan's wellingtons out as far as I could into the trees, knowing I wouldn't need them again. A heavy stream of traffic was heading south along the valley floor towards Manchester, and as I stood at the bus stop I felt it suck the air past, making its own current in the absence of real wind, tugging at my jacket, wanting me to go the same way.

Until the bus actually came, I must have been still kidding myself that something would turn up — something to break the momentum and free me from the consequences of all that I'd done and all that I'd failed to do. But then it was there and I was boarding it and straightaway the valley started breaking up around me into shitty homes and shops and a sea of traffic. The whole, awful mass of Greater Manchester reared up in minutes, swallowing every beautiful and good thing in the world. Until then, deep down, I must have still thought that I would get another chance to talk to Kate. But I was alone on that bus, as I had been coming, and Kate and Tom were already miles away, stuck in the mud on that hill, with Vic snoring away and the eaves leaking. Rain came in sheets over the bus and the streets now, like hard sheets of ice and snow, layers of an avalanche that would never stop separating us for the rest of our lives.

Even at the airport, even on the plane, until it actually lifted clear of the ground I somehow felt I could still go back. I could see red lights in the distance, glowing against the haze beyond, then in a swoop the whole grey mess of buildings and roads was pulled out from under my feet again. The green horizon itself dissolved into vapour. I felt a stab in my chest and huddled closer to the little window with my chin in my palm, watching grey cloud run its ragged course far below. Where it was torn and unmended, a more intricate needlework of grey, green and white land was running away slowly now, far below.

Out of nowhere came the clear memory of a photograph on a bookshelf in Kate's hallway. I hadn't even registered seeing it at the time, but now it was as if I stood there again, cheap carpet underfoot and the deep, faint rumble of Vic's snoring in the air.

It was a poor photo, taken too far away with a cheap camera, but it was Tom all right — a younger Tom with even shorter hair, a la Cantona, posing shamelessly in front of the house, displaying white teeth to please, with his eyebrows raised in an ironical gesture he could hardly even know the meaning of. It was a glimpse of a character I hardly knew — someone who knew how to please in order to get what he wanted, without wondering why it pleased, or where the pleasure lay. He had his United shirt on, with the collar up like Cantona and he knew it. That was half the smile: here I am. I could still recall the thrill of that, myself: the little man in the big shirt. Images receded into the past like opposing mirrors, of players living and dead: uncles, cousins and friends, old enemies and heroes. It was the picture of a lost dimension, a lost self.

The cloud was breaking up now, far below. We were already approaching the Channel. It was so easy, so fast. I could still see the soft undulations of land below, and the dark crevices where towns grew like mould. But as I watched, the sun showered the scattered clouds with bronze and the sea rose to the east. Then the water was growing and the land receding all the time, until only one last town protruded from one last strip of green. I watched the end of a tiny pier, clearly visible even at twenty thousand feet, as it slid under the shining wing of the plane like a blade of grass under a scythe. Then there was just the silver sea, bronze clouds and a grey wing. A moment later I looked out the window again, and there was nothing there at all.

# HALF-TIME"

*You cannot defend on your backside.*

Bobby Moore

# I

Vanessa agreed, without much persuasion, that coming to the airport was pointless. She had work to do anyway. So I faced the Perth dawn on my own, too tired to care. My eyes stayed open in the taxi, heading west down Leach Highway, but I was more asleep than I'd been on the plane with them shut. I registered the broad verges of dry grass and the tin sheds selling tractors and beds but I wasn't really there. I hadn't really landed. I saw the unbelievable breadth of the sky, and the whiteness of it soaking blue. On the outskirts of Fremantle, I saw the sun's first touch on the tips of the York gums, turning the leaves crimson, but I still didn't believe it. It was a dream — a hollow, familiar dream, and I just wanted to sleep straight through it.

When I woke later that morning, I saw a lot of white plaster and a freestanding steel clothes rack full of unironed shirts. On the other wall was a tattered poster of the Stone Roses falling asleep on stage. There were cedar blinds closed over the window to my right, leaking light, and if I opened them I knew I'd see a blank blue sky. So I didn't.

It was hot. I got up, got out and walked down Marine Terrace in bathers and an old Happy Mondays shirt, towel over my shoulder. All the buildings looked shabby and low, and vaguely disappointing. I crossed the park, then the rail line and walked on to the little beach hidden behind the limestone cliffs. Through the old whalers' tunnel cut into the cliff face I could see a glimpse of streets just as deserted as the beach. I swam out into the bay and looked back at the old limestone buildings and tin sheds as if I was yet to land, as if I could just swim away.

Back on the sand, resting against the cool face of the cliff, I let the slow, mild easterly wind dry me. Closing my eyes, I was up on Stan's farm again, with heavy wet stones in my hands and the wind biting. I saw clumps of grass twisted in upon themselves against the wind, down where they emerged from the thin layer of dark soil. I saw again all those wavering dry-stone walls, running like broken vertebrae over the deserted hillsides, slowly being beaten by time. How could Stan ever keep up? He was too old. Who would find new ways to make money up there, and keep the shabby little housing estates and retirement homes at bay?

The silence on the beach was shocking. I could hardly hear the sea shift on the sand, the air was so still. Overhead, the cliffs hung dangerously, fringed with saltbush and grass, yet their underside was bright with the glow from sunlit sand below. There wasn't a single patch of darkness there — the light found every crevice.

The planting program along the beach had progressed in my absence. They were revegetating the degraded dunes with native plants, trying to heal old wounds.

Never before had the sea looked so wide.

I was still there in the shrinking shadow of the cliff when a woman in a slender black suit appeared near McDonald's. She saw me, but she stood there on the low retaining wall for maybe three minutes before reaching down, plucking off her shoes and stepping onto the beach.

She trod the warm, fine sand as if it were wet mud, holding her shoes waist high. She didn't wave, she didn't smile and neither did I. I just went on sitting there, with my legs stretched out and a stubborn mist over my mind. All I could think was, 'Too soon, too soon.'

She'd cut her hair shorter than I'd seen it before, keeping the sharp horizontal fringe I'd always forgiven her for, knowing she hated her face without it. There was a neat cut high across her neck now; her face was pale against this dark line.

'I thought I might find you here,' she said, reaching the shadow of the cliffs. Her voice was softer and sweeter than it had sounded on the phone, and as my eyes adjusted, the uncanny perfection of her pale skin rose up out of the shadow. The curve of her lovely long neck.

'I knew you'd find me here,' I said.

The elegance was a complication I'd forgotten somehow. She stood before me, barefoot in a plain black suit, long pale toes poised an inch above the fine blonde sand, it seemed. As if she weighed nothing at all. She peered down at me, but narrow green glasses hid her eyes like a blindfold. 'So are you going to get up and give me a hug?' she said.

'Can't. Legs don't work.'

'Jetlag?'

'Feels worse than jetlag.'

'Jetlag always does, George. Come on: get up, for goodness' sake. I want to hear what you have to say.'

'Can't. The thing is, V, I don't have much to say.'

'Well, that's convenient, isn't it? For you, I mean. Less said the better, is it?' She sounded like a school teacher for a moment, and glared at me, but just as suddenly abandoned this, as if dissatisfied. 'George!' she said urgently. That's all: my name in warning, as if the cliffs were falling. And, as if they really were, I wanted to get up, reach out and pull us both clear, but in the mist of tiredness, grief and confusion it felt like one of those dreams, when you're paralysed at the crucial moment. As a kid, I used to dream of football that way: I'd have the ball at my feet and a good look at the goal and I just wouldn't be able to kick the damn thing in.

'I like it here,' I said. 'I can't face the rest yet.'

'We can't talk here, George.'

'Can we leave the talking, V? Just for today. Can we leave that out?'

She took off her glasses then and rubbed her eyes, and I felt something close to guilt. 'I'll be better tomorrow,' I said. 'I'll come and see you.' She continued to rub her eyes. 'Been working hard?' I asked.

'Harder than you.'

She turned her pale blue eyes on me then, and their brightness hit me like it always had. A blind man would have felt it, I swear — the visceral shock of blue eyes and white skin in the brilliant Fremantle sun; the fall of fabric over slender hips, shoes swinging, the whole thing.

'I still don't understand why you went. It was a bloody nasty thing to do, George. To me.'

I was seeing her in this blinding wash of light that left nothing hidden, yet magnified everything so that she seemed less real than ever. I knew this was wrong, but I couldn't help it. I was willing her to be silent and still, like the beach. I just wanted to look at her, as if I might puzzle it out that way, given time; as if the Vanessa I loved lived in the deep texture of her skin and clothes, in the growing ferocity of her eyes now, waiting, in the corrugations of her brow, hidden by her fringe. I saw her naked again, suddenly. Was this all I'd ever seen?

'Tomorrow, V. I'm sorry.'

'You don't sound very sorry.'

I had to look away, it was so true. I didn't feel half as sorry as I wanted to. I just felt numb. 'Are you home tomorrow?'

'I can be, yes.'

'Big reunion tomorrow, then. I'll bring some of that fizzy Tasmanian stuff you like.'

'Taltarni.'

'That's it.'

'Oh, all right.'

She didn't look belligerent or demanding any more, she merely looked resigned, in a way I couldn't recall. I sensed she'd just wanted to get it over with, to make it up between us and move on, whatever it cost her.

But that wasn't what I wanted. Neither did I want to fight. Anything but silence would be a betrayal or a lie now, it seemed.

It felt like we might never speak again, Vanessa and I, and the longer we left it, the more it seemed that every possible word we might exchange had already passed between us. What had we ever talked about anyway? I knew the answer to that. Me.

So Vanessa stared out to sea a bit longer, then she just walked off without speaking, with a weak little wave of her shoes. Which left me where she'd found me, watching her shrink to anonymity.

I hadn't even touched her.

'Home' was the house Vanessa had bought years before. It was an old house by local standards, in a leafy suburb close to the city, and it was to be our home after the wedding. We'd spent a small fortune getting it renovated and landscaped. Vanessa had been collecting bits and pieces for it since her aunt died, leaving her a bequest. She'd moved in alone then. We would live there together after the wedding, she said, and be happy.

Today it looked like every other house in the street,

distinguished mainly by a splash of purple on the gable and the tight-arsed front garden the landscape architect had left behind. I had to ring the bell, having no key as yet. After half a minute, locks and latches rattled inside, then the door swung open cautiously to reveal Vanessa in a short black dress that looked too good to sit around the house in. Lipstick too, I noticed, and a silver bracelet I'd never seen before.

She checked my face without speaking, pulled me through, then locked the front door again as if I might leave. She put her long slender arms out in a vulnerable way and I held her close, surprised at my own emotion. She was softer than I'd remembered and she folded against me with heartbreaking ease. We held on for a long time by our standards and when I kissed her lips it felt so good that for maybe five seconds I wanted to cry.

'Hi,' she said, very much Starting Afresh. We parted a little to share a cautious smile. I traced the lines of her ribs to her waist and nestled both hands on the cloth over her hips. It was a textured fabric of some kind, and it moved too easily over the silken lining beneath. She kissed me again, harder.

'That's better,' she said and pulled me closer behind my back.

'A chair, V,' I said. 'A chair and a cup of tea.'

'So where's the Taltarni?'

I shrugged, and let her go, angry already at the look on her face. 'Let's put the kettle on.' I moved past her down the corridor, past that bloody photo of her father, but when we got to the kitchen she pulled me up. 'What is it with you?' she said. 'Why do you have to be so difficult? Why can't you just —?' She shook her open hands in the air, lost for words.

'Sorry.'

'Yeah, right, and don't you sound sorry.' She went to the kettle while I sat down wearily on the far side of the table. 'And that accent! Honestly, George: you sounded like Whatsisname.' She was clicking her fingers again. 'I don't know: a famous Englishman.'

'Name one.'

She turned from the sink with narrowed eyes. 'You know what I mean.'

I nodded and smiled, but she kept right on looking at me. 'What?' I pleaded, palms up.

'Okay, for one: I want to know why you went away like that, and then I want to know why you've got so weird. Is there someone new?'

'No, there's no one new. Don't be ridiculous. I've just been on holiday, Vanessa. It's not so strange. Lots of people have them, you know, even if you don't. If you stopped work for five minutes, you'd probably like it too.'

The kettle began whistling politely. We both looked aside. 'Well, you're well-rested, I see.' she said, and turned the gas off. She didn't get cups out. 'Well,' she said, 'I'm waiting.'

'For?'

'Oh, for an apology, I suppose. An explanation. Anything'll do at this stage. Anything that'll stop me running off down Waratah Avenue screaming.'

This was the moment to tell the truth — to clear the decks and move on, to face up to what had to be said, and say it. More lies now would only divide us. Yet the moment had come too soon. It would always be too soon. I had no defence, no justification, only regret and a little lukewarm shame, maybe. It had been the same facing Kate, and the bitter humiliation of her response was still too sharp in my mind. How could I dare repeat it?

'I don't know what you're on about. I've had a holiday. I'm back. That's it.'

'Do you love me?' she asked suddenly, so quiet that it sounded like someone else altogether.

'I've answered that a hundred times, V.'

'What sort of an answer is that? So come on: do you?'

Vanessa's blue eyes shone. I'd seen her desperately unhappy asking this before, shouting even, but I'd never seen the intensity and focus that shone there now. Knowing what this cost her, seeing real warmth released in her, in desperation — well, it chilled my spine with hatred of my cold, stupid heart, knowing I'd never wanted this from her, and still didn't. Knowing she could break herself entirely, for my sake, and it wouldn't make me love her more. Yet if Kate hit me, I'd thank her. The unfairness of it moved me, yet the need in Vanessa's eyes could not.

To tell the truth was beyond me, so I just said 'Yes, V. I love you very much.'

She held the stare for maybe five seconds more, then said 'Good,' and took two cups down off the shelf. She ran a swift hand across her face and spooned out tea.

'You've got a few things to tidy up,' she said.

'Such as?'

'Such as keeping your job. Such as — don't look at me like that — sorting out your father's affairs.'

'Didn't know he had any.'

'You got a call last week. I've written it down somewhere.' She went and rummaged in her bag. 'Here it is. Ring this man — Roger Ferris. Here's the number.'

'But I don't want to ring Roger Ferris. Why on earth should I ring Roger Ferris? He's probably selling something.'

'No — he's a real estate agent —'

'There you go.'

'— and it's about your father's church.'

'I beg your pardon.'

'Your father's church. He owned a church. Didn't you know?'

'Didn't know he owned much at all, never mind a church. I know he never made the money he expected to. That's the only reason he came over here, you know, to get rich.'

'And isn't that terrible? And isn't it awful that you've inherited property?'

'It's a church, V. What am I going to do with a church, for God's sake?'

Vanessa leant forward with heavy patience. 'You're going to sell it, dear, and pay off our mortgage. That's what you're going to do.'

I rang Roger Ferris that afternoon and talked to Roger

147

Ferris and agreed to meet Roger Ferris at the property in question, two days hence. I ate the meal Vanessa made, poured a lot of wine into my glass and then just as easily poured myself into bed with Vanessa, swathed in the heart-rending softness of warm skin and new cotton sheets.

'Do you use a fabric softener?' I asked, but my heart was full, really. I felt this stupid urge to cry every time she touched me. And she touched me a lot. 'Did you wait for me?' I murmured drunkenly, and she laughed.

I felt the old current build of its own accord, from one end of my spine to the other, and it felt simple for a moment, as if my body might act of its own accord. Which would have been fine. 'I'm drunk,' I told myself, and remembered being pissed the first time we met, at a party. I just wanted to feel something then, and that's why I'd touched her.

Now, in her bed, I wanted to be in her, suddenly — on her, over her. I couldn't feel enough of her skin against mine, as if the gulf between us might dissolve in the sweat that mingled there. She threw her head back dramatically, long before it was credible, but the long white stream of her neck pulsed in the dim light and her back arched, her belly bucking under my palm until the current in my body grew sharp and absurd. It seemed comic, but only in a way that threatened to make me shout or cry.

I steadied myself, grew tentative, nudging into her, felt my thoughts catch up with me. I was struggling to remember Kate's body, and I couldn't. I didn't even know it now: she'd shed that skin. What scars, what signs recorded Tom's arrival? I hadn't even been there, didn't even know what she'd gone through, never laid a comforting hand on her spine. And yet I dared to feel disloyal now, pressing against the clean, willing breast of Vanessa.

Vanessa seemed strangely relieved in the morning, and stayed in good spirits all week, more pleased at the sight of me than any time I could recall, no matter what my mood. She was patient with me, and asked no awkward questions and it scared me in a way her brusque manner never had. She cooked me breakfast and said, 'We're going to be happy,' apropos of nothing. She used her Office Smile on me. She let me drive her BMW. She even smiled when she told me how to drive it. She didn't talk about work, she talked about the house and the wedding. She mentioned sad friends who didn't have partners. She even brought one around for me to observe first-hand.

'Poor Helen,' she kept saying before her friend arrived. 'It's so-o-o sad. Can't we fix her up? You must know someone. What about your friends?'

'Is it so important that she marry? It's not the nineteenth century, you know.'

But Vanessa seemed buoyed, if anything, by the universal dearth of men. 'She can't sleep at night, George. She's got that big house all to herself. And there's no one in the office unmarried, not her age anyway. Poor Helen,' she said again, and looked me up and down.

Helen and Vanessa had started at law school together, swotting up on torts while I was still smoking behind Chadderton train station. They'd seen a lot of each other over the last few weeks in my absence and talked now over dinner like flatmates again, full of office gossip. Then they made me listen while they talked shoes for maybe forty minutes.

This was as nasty as the new Vanessa got.

I went home to Fremantle most nights that week, needing time alone. I would walk down the road in the evening to clear my head and get something to eat. There were always people out on South Terrace, and the muffled cacophony of schmalzy jazz and louder bands across the road. The cafes were often half-empty inside, but their tables outside were full each night. If the traffic was light there was a subtler song to be heard, out there on the pavement — people tapping spoons and laughing, light sounds rising up into the dark sky like birdsong. Everyone seemed glad to be there.

So why couldn't I forget miserable Soppstone and miserable Kate, I asked myself. Why think continually of a woman you didn't really know, who had nothing but anger towards you, whose life was sad verging on hopeless, someone happily attached to the kind of guy you avoided outside nightclubs? Why think of her — why see her in the street every day — if she didn't give a shit, and Vanessa clearly did? Why, in the face of Vanessa's high spirits, dwell on someone who hated you, someone you'd never see again?

Because, I concluded. Just because. Because I felt

something. Because I wanted to know if she was all right, if Tom was all right, if it was still raining, or had cleared a bit. Because the very thought of our one conversation made me wince and turn suddenly, in the middle of South Terrace, as if to shake it from my head. That was the worst thing — speaking to her just once and doing it so badly. There was pointless pain there that cried out for a sequel.

Had she looked out for me, going back to school the next day? Did she still? Did she expect me to turn up again? Surely she'd expected me to try one more time ... Maybe she'd just been angry that first time. Maybe she'd regretted it later ...

I was stuck in a traffic island, halfway across the road, imagining Kate scanning the carpark for me, from under a dripping hood. I couldn't help it, I saw it so clearly — saw her round, dark eyes as if she were really there, as if she had already spoken to me, saying stay.

# II

Vanessa had told them to expect me at the office on the following Monday morning, and to my dismay they'd agreed, but I'd also arranged to meet Roger Ferris at the same time, somewhere out in the southern suburbs, and that seemed the least grim option. 'They'll just have to wait,' I told her. 'Alert New York.'

Vanessa wouldn't laugh at that — it was Sunday night by then and work loomed large, so Vanessa was a different woman. The fact of work precluded laughter, full stop. She readily let me go with an angry peck on the cheek, and I drove home, relieved to be on my own. We'd spent the whole weekend together and already it felt like I'd never been away. Whinely was a bad dream again. Everything had fallen back into place.

But the sun was in my eyes next morning as I drove eastward into dry suburbs and it splintered off silver foil crosses planted by the roadside, blinding me. They marked road deaths, these crosses — private tributes to dead strangers. Some flowers were wilting in the sun, I noticed. Others had long dried out. Only the plastic ones still had colour.

Roger Ferris was waiting in his car in a quiet, dry street in a quiet, dry suburb deep in the Pom Belt. I hadn't been there for years. My parents had built nearby soon after arriving, attracted by cheap land and English estate agents. Not that Mum ever got to see the lawn go down.

It being March, broad swathes of blond grass now lined the roads, all but the faintest trace of green having leached out over summer. It hadn't rained since September, Vanessa said, and the simple fact astonished me, as if it were unusual.

Roger Ferris emerged from his Statesman a good six inches taller than me. Glaring down under uncultivated eyebrows, he had a stoop which made him look predatory. 'You wish to ... inspect the property?' he asked, as if it were Windsor Castle, and swung a prodigious arm in a ceremonial arc, revealing a dark patch under his armpit.

In the middle of the corner block stood a flat salmon-brick hall, its roof so low it seemed to have bowed under pressure from the sky. All the houses around were the same, bringing the blue vacuum down until you wanted to stoop. We skirted the church, our shoes squeaking over the dry buffalo grass. There was only one window visible — a long horizontal slot at the eaves. A couple of ancient marris struggled on in the far corner of the block and in their shadow, half-buried in nuts and browning leaves, I spotted a discarded metal sign. 'Uniting Church Kenwick Parish' it read.

Roger Ferris was unlocking the main doors. 'Doesn't the church need it any more?' I asked.

'I wouldn't know about the church's affairs, Mr Fielden. That's their business, though you'd be surprised — there's always a couple of these on the market. You should get four units on this block, no problem. Your father had assurances from the council that rezoning would be no problem. Residential. R40.'

'Right. R40. Good.' R40 sounded fine, but I wasn't going to ask what it meant. Vanessa would know.

There was no aisle inside, or any kind of ornament or fancy window, just stacks of metal chairs at the far end where the altar must have been. 'The young 'uns don't go in for church much any more, eh? Can't blame 'em. We need to get a few more migrants in again. More migrants, fewer refugees, eh? That'll lift the market.' Roger Ferris stamped gingerly at the timber floor. 'Nice width board,' he said and walked out with his mobile phone chirping.

It was hot in the bare hall, and I had no reason to linger there, but I went down and looked at the papers piled on the chairs anyway. There was sheet music peppered with dead insects, and flyers for fetes that clearly hadn't raised enough to save the church. A copy of a sermon too, headed 'The Free Movement of the Spirit,' which seemed a bit wordy for Kenwick. It talked a lot about 'the gathered church,' which rang oh-so-faint bells from Sunday School at Chadderton Congregational. The Spirit charged us to seek other believers, apparently, and to 'walk together in church order,' whatever that meant.

Where had this congregation walked to now? Were the parishioners still together at all, in nursing homes and villas, or penned off individually in granny flats in their kids' back yards? How many had come from England — from Lancashire or Yorkshire? Had all that drive and resilience found its dead-end here, a couple of years ago, on a hot Sunday morning?

Vanessa was thrilled with R40. It meant we wouldn't have a mortgage, she said. And if I didn't turn up to work on Tuesday morning, I wouldn't have a job, she said, so I took the seven-thirty train to Perth and talked to men I'd hoped never to see again.

Everyone pretended I'd never been away, and asked about Vanessa. By nine o'clock I was at my desk on the fifteenth floor again, staring at an empty calendar and a view of the Swan estuary so static that it looked like wallpaper stuck to the glass. Beyond Perth Water, flat suburbs receded to a hazy blur. It felt like years since I'd sat there. Literally years.

'One call at a time,' I told myself. 'Just one call after another. Easy does it.' I filled out my time sheet ten minutes at a time, knowing it would be an issue in a fortnight, when they added it all up, but could not be an issue today. I heard myself on the phone, authoritative, dismissive or sycophantic as required, and I looked on in wonder, not sure how I did it. How I'd ever done it.

'Didn't think you were coming back,' Dave Hackett said, and it was a joke.

'Where else would I go?'

Where else indeed? Who else would I be? What else was I qualified to do? This was my slot: a slot I'd worked hard for these past ten years with a singleness of purpose that astonished me now. Back there, at Stan's, it had felt like I was twenty-one again and free to choose. What a spell that place had held over me. What an illusion it all seemed now, with my bum in the same blue swivel chair, and a pile of familiar files before me that might stay with me for years.

Everything was set up. All I had to do was to play my part. The trouble was I could see ahead, to the wedding and beyond. Decades of dull work stretched out before me, decades of timeserving. I could see myself grown dull and cynical, whingeing at dinner parties until Vanessa wondered why she had married me. Even when I thought of children, I imagined them a burden, with Vanessa even quitting work maybe, and me more trapped than ever.

I had engineered this situation — it was of my making as surely as if I'd planned it, ever since the day I left England and Kate. I'd set my course back then. This was just the arrival.

On Friday night, Vanessa and I drove to Helen's place, a small house in Dalkeith impressively close to the river but pretty basic really, an image of modest privilege from more egalitarian times. Helen had bought it when she was still a student working weekends, before the last property boom, but she hadn't managed an extension yet, lacking a second income.

'Poor Helen,' Vanessa said. 'She'll never get the additions done. Not sleeping with married men, anyway. I know she's not happy. She always wanted children.'

'She's not sixty, V. You never know, she might disappoint you yet. She might have dozens of kids.'

'You can be so nasty at times. I don't want kids. We could have a dog, though. I'd like a dog.'

'That's it, then. My future life in Perth.'

Vanessa turned to me then, and slapped my hand softly on the steering wheel. 'You've had nothing but complaints about this place since you got back. People are always like that when they've been travelling.'

'But I think it's fine here. It's a damn sight finer than where I've been, I know that.'

'Oh, but nothing's really good enough, is it? It's too hot or too dull or the food's only ordinary or the beer's too cold. I'm getting a bit sick of all that, to be honest, George. I don't need that every day.'

'I just said —'

'It was the way you said it — like every day was the same. It can't be so bad if you've lived here so long.'

'It's not the place. The place is not the point, is it?'

'Oh? What is the point, then?'

I parked the car. Helen's house was only across the street, but this was dangerous territory all the same and like that drunk in the minefield I wasn't sure how I'd got there. 'I don't know, V. Don't know if there is one.'

'Is it me? Am I the point? Is that what you're trying to say?'

'No, no.' I could hardly return her look, she seemed so exposed. 'Maybe it is the place, after all. Not that there's anything wrong with it, but maybe some of us aren't meant to move at all. Do you know what I mean, V? Maybe for some of us there can't be a second place, like we're married to the first or something, y' know? Without knowing it, we've made a ... a pact.'

'Married?'

'No. Forget it, V. It doesn't matter. It's all bullshit. I don't know what I mean.'

'That makes two of us.'

The champagne cocktails were a mistake — I knew that as soon as I drank the fourth, because the table wouldn't keep still. It was twelve at the table and Vanessa and I chose opposite ends, having a long-standing agreement that the conversation 'ran smoother' that way. I had Helen on my left and directly opposite a bloke called Tim, whose spectacles were smaller than his eyes, I swear. Tim took it upon himself to make conversation, clearly a skill he'd learnt in the courtroom.

'So, George: tell us about this retreat to the wilds of Olde Englande,' he said, with glances across the table. 'Where did you stay? How long were you there? How come you didn't take our Vanessa?'

'I've never met the Defendant in my life,' I said.

Helen laughed circumspectly — Tim was single — and put a hand on mine to shut me up. It was surprisingly soft, Helen's hand. 'A farm, Vanessa said?' she coaxed. 'Was it one of those Bed and Breakfast places?'

'No. My uncle's place.'

'I can't honestly imagine you on a farm, George,' she said.

'I was there to catch up with family, really. It was just somewhere to stay.'

'Are your parents in the UK?' asked Tim, peering at me through his tiny lenses. 'Is that it?'

'No. They migrated here.'

'Ah! Now, if I was an immigrant,' Tim announced, swallowing wine, 'I would just draw the line. Like that.' Tim indeed drew a vertical line in the air between us with a slice of his hand. 'I mean, what's the point in coming all this way just to keep going back? I mean — I don't mean you, George — are they Australian or not? They just have to —' again the hand '— draw the line and forget Italy or bloody Iraq, eh?'

'Why do I invite you, Tim?' Helen wailed. 'Honestly.'

'I mean, if it's so awful where they've come from … These refugees, for instance — they want the easy life, so they run away to Australia, then they expect us to keep them. I mean, it's just typical.'

'Who hasn't run away from something?' I demanded, fixing Tim with a wine-heavy stare. 'We just call it looking for a better life. Why crucify some poor bloody bastard from Iraq when you'd do exactly the same in the same situation? This whole bloody country is full of people doing that, always has been, only we call it the good life, or dropping out, or getting on, settling down. Accumulating. It's all the same. Houses, cars, marriages, mortgages — they're all built on fear, just the same. Fear of the big wide world.'

'Pretty bleak view of life, isn't it?' Helen protested.

Tim leant back in his chair. 'Well, spot the fiancée,' he teased and Helen told him pretty smartly to shut up, precipitating a general hush.

I saw Vanessa's head go down, and later caught Tim glancing smugly my way over the main course, as if weighing up the evidence for the prosecution. I was weighing up what it would cost me to break his smug face open. I don't know what we talked about after that, or how much I said. I only know that the wine was irresistible, that it took a lot to drown my anger — a lot of talk, a lot of wine — and that Vanessa wasn't at the table towards the end, nor Helen. When Helen brought her back, Vanessa's eyes were red, as if she'd cried over someone. The first time we met, she'd looked like that, at that party, and she'd worn a bright red dress. I remembered now. Someone had just left her, then. Poor V.

Vanessa drove me away in my own car, so I guess the wine worked. I woke up in the middle of the night fully dressed in Vanessa's spare room, in a narrow bed. Damp sheets were tangled around my legs. It wasn't that hot, but the window was closed and the room was small and I was sweating, and I knew precisely what it meant, being placed there.

I kicked at the sheets, and they tightened. I rolled out of bed onto the cool timber floor, kicking again until I heard them tear.

'Shit!'

I had to get out — out of the sheets, out of the room, out of the house altogether. The walls were spinning, the room was dark and somewhere there was bile wanting to surface.

My shoes were still on — another bad sign. I stepped out into the silent corridor, under the horrible portrait of her horrible dead dad. The most direct part of Vanessa had always seemed tied to him, trapped in the past, leaving just the remainder to deal with everyday love — with me, in other words, or any other inadequate man she found. And the worst of it was, this was the thing about Vanessa that was most raw and real — this wholehearted attachment to a dead man, who'd have hated me, had we ever met.

I crept towards the front door, where the keys would be. There was coloured glass in the doorway and sickly yellow light bleeding through at my feet. I stared at it, frozen to the spot: I was in Tom's house, in the corridor hearing Vic's snore. More: I was Tom himself, tiptoeing past so as not to wake Vic, remembering not to flush the toilet, nursing bruises, wondering if Mum was home.

The keys were glinting in yellow light, and it was snow on black rock, flecks of quartz catching moonlight. It was foil on a cross on the side of the road catching the sun. It was frost on an empty bottle in the mud where Stan now lay freezing.

I had a cold sweat on me, head to foot. I wanted to piss, I wanted to throw up, I wanted to run. I was cowering in the hallway of my future home, trying to run away again. How could I forget, when it was still happening, still daylight there in the middle of the night? How could I forget a damn thing?

# III

I got drawings in the post eventually, courtesy of Roger Ferris, showing the planned development in Kenwick. I wasn't sure what to do with them, but Vanessa wasn't around to ask, in fact I hadn't seen her since the night at Helen's. She was preparing a case at home and wouldn't be in the office until Monday, they said. For ten long days I hadn't quite called her house.

The plans showed four tight little retirement villas with courtyards smaller than their bathrooms. That morning at work, contravening office guidelines, I rang the number beside the architect's name and a girl put me through. 'The scale's out,' I said. 'They're designed for pygmies. Is it pygmies you had in mind?'

Peter Warner, architect, wasn't amused, and he'd clearly gone to a better school than I. 'The brief from your father was very explicit,' he said, making it sound dirty. 'A two-storey development would never get approval, so —'

'Put three homes on, then. Or two.'

'But you'll make much less money. You're aware of that?'

'How much?'

He told me.

'That'd still be enough,' I said.

There was a long pause at the other end of the line, then a cough. 'I'll take a look at the changes you've suggested,' he said. 'There's no doubt it'll work better. We might even save the marris.'

'Yes, do that. Save the marris, for God's sake.'

'We can still make the committee meeting with amended plans, if you can approve the changes by the twelfth. Now, what is it today?'

'April fifth,' I said and just dropped the phone dead then and there, hearing myself say it. April fifth. The day Tom was born.

I invented an appointment which the secretary didn't believe, and got out of the building fast. I broke more guidelines down at the car pool and drove down to Leighton Beach, where the first cloud cover since I'd got back was spreading the glare evenly across the sky and turning the sea hard green. I parked the car opposite the dunes and sat there for a long time, knowing I should be at the office, knowing all the crises that were building there, knowing the chop loomed overhead as surely as the sun. Knowing it was Tom's tenth birthday.

I must have fallen asleep there in the carpark, calculating time differences, because I heard the rain before I was fully awake. I listened to it rumbling overhead and drilling against the window, and I saw very clearly in my head silver light gathering in lines of muted radiance across the sky, turning green to grey and grey to green again, until I couldn't tell them apart. Greys shone over the valleys, the stone towns and the woods, all the way to the sea.

Underneath the sound of the rain I could hear the blades of the wind farm scooping hollows in the wind, and the blades of loose grass flowing like water up the slopes. I heard rain falling lightly everywhere around me, and felt the enclosure protecting me: walls and roof drawn for me in sound. I could hear where they were — it was a tiny room, a dark room, a cool one.

Then I heard a child laughing and that was right too, but it woke me properly and when I opened my eyes the light was painful. Two girls were under a beach shower in their bathers, laughing at their dad, who was flicking them gently with a wet towel.

Given a sympathetic ear, I might have said I was tired. I might have said I didn't belong there. But no one asked. No one ever had. I thought of maybe Mum, but no, not really: a sympathetic presence, at best, with an ear out for Dad. Someone with flour on her apron. If she touched your hair the gentleness shocked you, but that was all. No wise counsel, just too much damned acceptance for anyone's good.

What, who, was I waiting for? I couldn't have said, but I grew aware of an overwhelming sense of grief, sitting there alone in the car: grief for all the silent nights when I hadn't been woken by a baby's cry or a child's bad dream; grief for all the fights I'd never had, all the fights and fears worth having, all the tears worth shedding.

I was thinking of Tom, as I always seemed to be now, but I was also thinking of Bob in the Throttled Hen, settling into the padded corner of that wood-panelled room as dim and hushed as a church. I thought of the bitter comfort of the beer going down and of having someone there to hear my worst. I heard Bob's stubborn order, out in the cold carpark: 'Go home,' he'd said. 'Go home.'

I drove to Vanessa's house, knowing I'd be at least expected, if not exactly welcome. Vanessa greeted me at the door with little enthusiasm, yet her scowl was part theatrical, and I could see her already feeling her way beyond it, wanting to be happier with me, to laugh even. That was Vanessa's gift — the desire to be happy, the determination to bounce back every time. That's how we stayed together.

'There's a package,' she said, trying to sound bored. 'In the Parlour.'

'Do we have to call it that?'

'No, we can call it the Sheep Dip if that makes you feel better. Here.' She put a hand on a cardboard box the size of a microwave. 'Were you expecting something?'

'I wouldn't get too excited,' I said. 'I've bought nothing. Maybe it's those files on the McGregor case.'

'But they're English stamps.'

They were indeed, and the postmark said 'Oldham.' My heart leapt in a painful way, but only my heart knew why.

'Well: open it.'

'You're sure? I could leave it —'

'Oh, come on.' Vanessa produced a sturdy pair of scissors from her pocket and had a go at the heavy brown masking tape. Some of the tape had already been cut, I saw. Vanessa wasn't one to wait. 'Come on: rip it.'

The first thing I pulled out of the bubble wrap was the cheap tea set Alice had offered me in her bedroom, what seemed like months before. 'Oh!' sang Vanessa. Then, seeing it clearly, with the silver paint peeling, a lower note: 'Oh.'

Under the teapot were souvenir teaspoons and the glass vase that would never come clear, I knew. 'That stubborn old woman,' I muttered. My hands shook, touching the spoons. 'I told her. I told her I didn't want her bloody junk.'

'It's not that special, is it?' Vanessa agreed. 'Still, you can put it in one of those charity bins.'

'It belongs in a bin, all right. It's junk, V.'

'All right, all right. What are you so upset about?'

I couldn't say. Maybe it was the sadness of what Mum had left behind. Maybe it was just the persistence — the sheer bloody persistence of these women, doing 'the right thing' no matter what. It all seemed so pointless.

'I don't mind this.' Vanessa held a cream and mustard porcelain gravy boat that might have been my grandmother's.

'Vanessa, you don't make gravy.'

'I might. Here.' She pranced across the room brightly and placed the gravy boat on a high shelf over the fireplace, between a porcelain boot and a picture of someone else's father. 'That's nice. That's Heritage, isn't it?'

For maybe five seconds I stared at Grandma's gravy boat marooned on Vanessa's shelf, then I pulled it down and threw it back in the box, rattling against the teapot. I picked up the box, took it out to the back and threw it in the big green bin where it belonged.

I came back theatrically fencing palms, trying to look satisfied. Vanessa was where I'd left her, and she didn't look at me. She just glanced at the empty table and the shelf on the wall. I'd never seen such anger in her face before. 'It's just junk, V,' I pleaded. 'They're just objects. All this.' I spun arms about, taking in the whole room, the whole house, the whole world. 'It's just objects, things. They don't mean anything. They don't matter.'

Vanessa cast hooded eyes my way. She was turning the engagement ring on her finger as if it might come off. 'You've no respect, have you?' she said.

'For what? For Grandma's gravy pot? It's just a thing. This is just a house, V.'

'Funny,' she said, 'I thought it was our home.'

She stormed out to the big green bin, of course, and I couldn't bear to watch. I left. When I visited again there'd be a gravy boat on the shelf.

How quickly any generosity or affection for Vanessa could turn to pure irritation, I thought, driving home. How little leeway I gave her after all — the smallest thing could make me furious, as if every straw were the last. What was this temptation to hurt her, this impulse to strike out? Had it been there before? I supposed it had, but I couldn't bear it any more — couldn't bear the self-contempt it bred, either.

I was still angry about the bloody gravy boat when I got back to Freo, and I tried Alice's number straightaway. When I got no reply, I couldn't resist the excuse to call Stan. I let it ring a good few minutes, knowing he wouldn't hurry, and knowing the old phone had a healthy ring that even Stan couldn't ignore forever. Eventually, sure enough, the tone clicked and I heard breathing.

'Stan? Is that you, Stan? This is George.'

'Who?'

'George. George Fielden. Your — Bloody hell, don't do that, Stan. Why do you do that?'

'Oh, it's worthwhile if it bothers you so.'

'You all right? You sound a bit rough.' He sounded pissed, was what he sounded.

'Are you ringing about your aunty?'

'Yes. Look: she's sent me this terrible pile of rubbish, Stan. I've a good mind to send it back. She's such a stubborn old —'

'Have you caught Roy? No, no you haven't, have you? She's passed away, George. That's it. That's why they've sent y' mother's things on.'

'She's what?' I'd heard it but it was just words. Alice was still wheezing in her armchair where I'd left her. They were all just where I'd left them. But then I remembered her red face, desperate for air, trying to laugh off the pain.

'It were quick, lad, in the end, and not even Roy saw it coming, like. She weren't in hospital more than a day. You know how she was — she wouldn't go in for love nor money.' The line crackled a bit. Stan coughed, a heavy, horrible cough.

'When was that, Stan? When's the funeral?'

'Come and gone, lad, this Tuesday. I called, but you're never in.'

'You could have left a message. Why didn't you leave a message?'

'Oh, I don't go in for machines. It'll be our Roy that's sent those things on.' Stan coughed again, and it had an edge to it this time. 'She were all right, our Alice. She were a gradely lass, for all her faults.'

'Are you all right, Stan?'

'Of course I'm bloody all right. Oi, this must be costing you. Are you timing this?'

'No Stan, I'm not timing it.'

'Bloody hell. I'll be seeing you then, lad. All right?'

The line died and the static with it. I was thinking 'Stan's the last one,' thinking he would die and so much die with him, useless drunken whinger that he was. One more call, one more cardboard box in the mail, and that was it.

Tom, too: he was caught up in the fate of those old timers, though he didn't know it. He'd never even know they'd been born.

That night it rained at last, loud on the tin roof, and I dreamt that I was up on the moors in the rain, heading for Tom's house. I reached the high rocky rise before the last hill, but the stones were slippery and steep and I kept slipping. I knew if I made the rise, I'd see the house, and I'd know then that they were home and safe. But when I made the rise and looked, there was nothing there.

For weeks after that I carried around some kind of conviction I couldn't pin down, and it came from the dream somehow. Something to do with the obsessive need to clear that rise, to the exclusion of all else. On Saturdays I stayed home and caught up on work, instead of ringing Vanessa as I knew I ought. She didn't ring me, either. When the backlog of paperwork subsided, I cleaned the bathroom and the kitchen, and sang along to the radio. I'd be going along fine, then find myself weeping like an idiot to something moribund like 'Yesterday', or just staring into space.

Finally unpacking the suitcase I'd left open on my bedroom floor, I found a rounded river stone I'd brought back as a paperweight. I squeezed it in my fist and held its flat edge against my forehead. It felt cool, cold even, and the cold seemed to come from the heart of the stone. It was hard, too — the muscles in my hand, clasped tightly as they were, felt soft and pliable around the uncompromising stone. A country is made of little more than this, I thought. It's no wonder that I'm tired. There's something like that in me, something hard and heavy that I've carried back with me. That's what makes my steps so heavy, even in May.

The weather was cooler now at least, and I got to wear

more than a shirt that night, having recovered my jacket from the suitcase. Vanessa had us booked for a dinner party at Deb's house, close to the university. I drove the long way there, between the campus and the river, as we often had in the years since graduating. Vanessa had even tried to persuade me along to alumni gatherings, where the intelligentsia would get together to examine wine and cheese for an hour or more. To 'keep up the connection,' she said, as if our own relationship depended on it — as if one might die without the other.

She made me pull the car in opposite the Law Building, apparently in no more hurry than I to arrive at Deb's. 'Seems a long time ago now,' I said.

'Don't be silly. It's only, what, five years since you left? Stop playing the old man. Anything's possible yet.'

I looked at her and the whole history of those years now shone in her blue eyes, overwhelming me with a sense of nostalgia and of lost time. I could no longer separate Vanessa from the unexpected promise of those days, from the contrast between my workaholic father's empty house and the sunny campus that Vanessa and I had explored between lectures. We seemed happy enough then. I wanted to ask her, 'What did we talk about, then?' but was afraid she'd say, 'You. We always talked about you.' Maybe Vanessa just couldn't find it in her to do that any more.

Even now it was a mystery just what had drawn her to me. I'd asked more than once, but my bewilderment pleased her too much and she'd just say, 'Must have been your bottom.' Back then, just the sweet old word 'bottom' seemed enough reason to care in return. I was that easily satisfied. I expected so little. It was mainly gratitude on my part, at first — gratitude for unexpected gifts.

As if reading my thoughts she asked the old question again.

I smiled at her anxious face. 'Yes I love you, V. God help me, I do.'

She laughed, but it died and she looked sadder than ever.

We were both quiet in the car after that, as if we'd argued, and once we got to Deb's we parted at the table with particular relief. I didn't know the crowd well — they weren't lawyers, they didn't like lawyers, and I couldn't blame them. I didn't like lawyers myself. I didn't know a lawyer who did. Vanessa had been in a bookclub with them, and she was already talking about books she hadn't read and abusing other people, not me, which I didn't mind at all. I heard Dean say, 'The first half was better than the second,' and I settled in for a long night.

The wine felt good and the food was superb, so I let silence creep up on me, not having anything to say. Office politics and sport left me cold anyway. What did I care about clothes and recipes and holidays in Italy or Bali? All I cared about, I realised, was a sodden, hopeless hill where such pleasures weren't exactly on the menu.

I hadn't told Vanessa about Alice's death. I knew she wouldn't care. At the far end of the table, she was expounding plans to buy a holiday home in the south-west, where she'd bring all her friends when it got too hot in Perth. Like Sandra's place but better, she hinted, and Sandra smiled back. I registered vaguely that it was my money she was spending, but the wine had its way and I leant back and smiled too.

There was a lump in the inside pocket of my jacket though, bothering me. I pulled out a folded piece of paper, muddied and torn. It was Tom's paper aeroplane — the one he'd thrown into the trees. I unfolded it, but water had smudged the ink and I was further than ever from being able to read it.

I had Helen by my side again, and she watched my lips moving until she couldn't bear it any longer. She took the paper from me in a swift swoop, before I could stop her. She read the childish script and looked at me with kindness I hadn't recognised before. 'Un artiste, à mes yeux, c'est celui qui a le don d'éclairer une chambre noire,' she intoned in quiet, mellifluous French.

Vanessa was listening intently to Mark, who'd chosen to be charming. I leant against Helen's bare shoulder and whispered, 'Meaning?'

Helen flicked hair from her dark eyes, weighing me up. Then she said, even more quietly, 'An artist, in my eyes, is someone who has the gift to light up a dark room.'

When this sank in, I stood up abruptly, knocking the table with my leg. Everyone turned to stare at the quiet one. 'Is it the meringue?' Rose asked. 'Is the meringue okay?'

'Sorry,' I said, to no one in particular, and walked up

174

behind Vanessa. She didn't turn or look back up at me. 'I have to go,' I said.

'What, now? Why?' Vanessa still didn't turn, pleading reason more to Rob and Victoria than to me. 'It's only ten o'clock.'

I leant down to face her, bending my knees, and she had to look at me at last. 'I'm sorry, V. I have to go,' I said quietly. 'I have to go to England.'

Her face changed in a way I knew I would carry with me for the rest of my days. Something gave way in her face in a physical way, and it scared and hurt me and it made me hate myself. A few seconds later she stood up oh-so-wearily and stepped away from the table. As we walked back through the house together, making excuses to Deb, Ros emerged from the kitchen with a bottle of champagne in one hand and a baby monitor in the other.

'Where are you guys going?' she asked, but quietly, and we could only walk on silently ourselves down the hall, letting children sleep on behind every closed door.

Within three minutes we were in the parked car, staring at the windscreen with nowhere to go. I told her about Alice. She didn't say anything. I told her Stan's health worried me. She just looked at her hands and told me to driver her home.

I drove back the short way and we both took an exaggerated interest in the traffic and the lights. When we stopped in her drive she opened the door, but just sat there staring ahead. 'Don't think I'm surprised,' she said. 'I'm not.'

'No.' She didn't sound it.

'You're just not serious, are you? You're not serious about marriage, any more than about work, are you? You never were. You can't put the time in, can you? You can't follow through, when you set on something, someone ...'

She took a deep breath, and I had nothing to say to fill the awful silence. 'You know this is it?' she said. 'You know that, don't you? We're not going through all this again, you know that?'

'I suppose so. It doesn't have to be that —'

'You're such a fucking bullshitting bastard, George. I can't listen to your bullshit any more.'

'Come on, V. We don't need to do this. We are who we are. We can't change now.'

'And when did you ever give me the chance? When did you ever make a suggestion, or say what you wanted, or what you liked about me? It takes two to change, George. I thought we might do that together. Instead, you just sit back and judge me all the time. I've seen it. You're doing it now.'

'I care for you, V. You know that. We just have the wrong things in common. We just want to be safe and not lonely or whatever.'

Vanessa's eyes narrowed to slits at this, as if she was seeing me for the first time, and I was very, very small. 'Is that how you see me?' she said, and I could hear the shock in her voice. 'Because I wanted you? Because I had the guts to stand by you, and put up with your bloody games all this time? That makes me some kind of coward?'

'I didn't say that. I don't think that. I'm sorry, V.'

'God, listen to us,' she said abruptly and got out, shutting the door hard. 'You've got to go, remember?' she said impatiently. 'So go. Just don't come back, George. Don't you ever come back.'

# SECOND HALF

*Mon Papa, c'est moi.*

Zinedine Zidane

I

Tom had his arms out at right angles to his body, and as he turned, one arm dipped like a wing, shuddering slightly in the gale, straight yet not entirely rigid, while his skinny legs trundled over rock and peat. The wind blustered and bullied him and he lifted and fell with it as if weightless, pushing off boulders and bending his knees. And always at his feet he wheeled the big white ball under him as if attached to it, the way I'd seen great footballers do. He glided away in the tide of the wind, endlessly celebrating an endless goal, endlessly waiting for the rough embrace of his team-mates.

But his gestures were too big for him, like the ball — overstated, melodramatic, straining to match his imagination. He'd been the same on the pitch, all his energy going into the drama rather than the effect.

He span away now from where I stood amongst the trees, not seeing me, not expecting me anyway, ever again. He moved to shoot, pulling his leg back with a wind-tortured shrub as his goal, arms spread like a dancer. At the final instant, though, he hesitated infinitesimally — I hadn't seen it before, but it had been there, I now realised — hesitated just enough to take the sting from the ball and send it wide.

The shrub, untouched, danced a mocking dance in the wind. Tom stared at it, then set off wearily downhill to retrieve the ball.

Signs of spring were few and far between in the carpark of the Betty Boothroyd Adult Advancement Centre. There wasn't any snow about — it felt too cold for that — there was just plenty of rain. I had to stand under the dripping eaves of the Halifax Building Society across the road for maybe an hour, with only the vaguest recollection of when Kate would be likely to turn up. In the end, I was lavishing so much attention on my poor sodden feet, and on trying to keep my case dry, that I almost missed her. A bus pulled up and there was just a flash of familiar yellow umbrella as half a dozen women made their way to the glass doors of the centre. She was in before I realised. So much for catching her going in.

Kicking myself angrily off the dark stone wall, I made my slow, reluctant way through the heavy traffic and crossed the carpark that had haunted me for months while I was away — the carpark I'd never wanted to see again, but had known I must, if I were to get through the next fifty years or so.

The lime green reception desk was empty, and looked

like it might have been empty since 1979. I could hear nasal voices echoing down the corridor to my right, so I followed, case in hand, listening to the squelch of my boots on the lino and the aggressive, ironic laughter of women I couldn't see but felt I had known all my life.

The second room coming off the corridor was long and bright and very, very cold, with skid marks on the lino. At the far end, beyond empty trestle tables, a dozen women stood with their backs to the door, talking. They were gathered in a tight arc, looking down at something I couldn't see.

I knocked and they turned and parted, to reveal two other women seated at computer terminals. These two women now stared back, like all the others, at the intruder. 'Could I speak to Kate Turner, please?' I said. 'Is there a Kate Turner in this class?'

Heads turned and Kate reluctantly stepped forward from the back, in a black and green jumper old enough for me to remember. 'Who's your admirer?' someone joked, and a couple of women laughed.

'Does he teach? Is he that new art teacher?'

'Doesn't look like an art teacher.'

'He's got that going for him, I'll say that.'

'Look: he's got his luggage.'

'Running off with y' lover, are y', Kate?'

Kate marched at me without responding and I backed out into the corridor, seeing her face. She followed and closed the door. 'You seem a bit short of computers,' I said. 'Funding, I suppose.' Kate looked at me, put a finger to her teeth and bit the nail. 'Government spending has to rise,' I said, trying to hold her gaze despite the contempt I saw there. 'The tax base has to broaden.'

'What do you want?'

It felt like she'd hit me, her voice was so harsh. 'Nothing. To talk. That's all I want. I really think we should talk.'

'And what for? To what end?'

'Oh, I don't know.' I looked about, up and down the empty corridor, as if the answer might be there. 'Didn't you look for me — be honest — next time you came here after running into me, didn't you look for me? Didn't you expect to speak to me again?'

'No.'

'Oh.' I sat the case at my feet, nursing a sore hand. Kate stared at it. 'Five minutes, Kate. Can that be so hard?'

'There's not a lot to discuss.' She put a hand on the door to the classroom then and took a last look at me.

'You know that's not true, Kate.'

'Tell me what, then. Tell me what we have to discuss.' It was a challenge, a parting shot.

'We have a child, Kate. We have a child to discuss.'

But her face went red hearing this and she moved away through the doorway. Turning, she spat out in a whisper, 'No. I have a child, George. You have a fucking nerve. Just piss off out of it,' and she slammed the door shut, just hard enough to scare me.

I caught a taxi to Stan's, not brave enough to face the bus

and the walk. I was anxious to get there, anyway: to sleep after a long flight and a long wait in the rain, but also to check on Stan. He'd stopped answering the phone weeks before. He didn't even know I was coming.

I stood in the wet yard and let the grumble and crunch of the taxi fade to a rumbling tone in the distance, rising and falling as it took the turns of the steep descent down the combe. There was no rain, for once, but the eaves were still thudding into the gravel all around, so it hadn't been clear for long. The farm seemed unnaturally quiet, as if violence had just passed, the air the stillest I could recall up there. The whole place seemed to be holding its breath, watching and waiting. Nothing more than the odd sparrow stirred, nudging the elms at the end of the road.

It was like a picture, or a dream — like I hadn't returned at all, like I couldn't, ever. I was looking at a photograph instead, but Stan wasn't in it.

Knocking on the front door got me nowhere, but spray was drifting down from the Pike now, so I pushed my way in and dumped my case in the hall. 'Anyone home?' I called, and thought I heard steps from the lounge.

The smell hit me first, going through. I was used to it in the fields, but it seemed much worse in that small darkened room. I walked over to pull the curtains, and a sharp shout of protest and sudden steps behind me made me whirl around. At first I thought there was something huge there, something monstrous. I was quite mad for a second, before I tugged curtains open and saw maybe twenty damp, muddy and complacent sheep standing in Stan's parlour.

They jeered me then, stirred by the light, defying me to turf them out. The carpet I now saw was peppered with shit, most of it well ground in. I opened the window just to breathe, then I pushed through the mass of fleece, but it panicked and split, half heading for bed and half for breakfast. I opened the kitchen door and shooed most of the sheep over the step, going out with them into the yard to check that the gate was shut. Upstairs, I found the ringleader backed in beside the cistern. He didn't look any more intelligent than the others, but he had a kind of grim determination written on his face that I had to respect. He reminded me of Stan.

I negotiated his withdrawal after a bit of skating about on shitty tiles, and the rest of the sheep followed. Then I went looking for their Uncle Stan, hoping to God he wasn't outside somewhere, half-dead. I found him in his own bed, but he was sharing it with two of the younger sheep — last year's lambs that Stan had been too sentimental to sell. They were the only thing worth selling on the whole hopeless farm.

The lambs jumped for it, seeing the game was up, but Stan slept on in the bouncing bed with his arms and legs outstretched like a compass, as only the drunk and the mindless can. His mouth was open, his face was pale, and I could tell from the smell he'd been drinking again.

I didn't have the heart to wake him. His breathing was fine and he'd be no use if he woke anyway. I just grabbed the scotch bottle near the bed, threw a blanket over him and went back to the kitchen to put the kettle on. Cleaning up was beyond me — I hadn't slept for forty-eight hours, and for nights before that I'd been half-awake running Vanessa and Kate and all the rest of it through my head, endlessly rehearsing things I'd said or hadn't said; times I'd lied when I should have told the truth, times I'd have been better off lying ...

I sat on the kitchen doorstep, which remained miraculously free of shit, and drank tea, watching the light fail. After checking Stan one last time, I dragged my case over to the little stone cottage which now seemed the closest thing I had to a home. The interior was wonderfully sheep-free and clean, and I just climbed straight into bed and slept.

Next morning I found Stan on his feet raking his parlour floor. He nodded at the carpet to welcome me, frowning and tugging at the big timber rake.

'Not surprised to see me then, Stan?'

'No, well ... someone put the sheep out, didn't they?' He didn't look a lot better than the night before, and seemed a bit shaky on the rake, but his nose was a healthy scarlet, at least, and he was sober enough to be embarrassed about what he was having to do.

'What on earth were they doing in there in the first place?'

Stan stopped the rake, leant on it a wee bit and stared out the front window. 'They're burnin' 'em, George,' he said and I could see his eyes were wet. 'They're burnin' every sheep within fifty mile of here, for fear of some disease or other. You can smell it when the wind shifts and it's a right pong, too.'

'But shouldn't you —'

'Oh, they'll find 'em soon enough.' The raking recommenced, to little visible effect. 'I don't know what I hoped to achieve. Felt sorry for 'em, I suppose. They're never meant for market, lad, most of 'em. I've had 'em for years. Butlin's Holiday Camp for sheep it is, up here. I've told you before: there's no future in this. I just want to be left to it. I won't be here forever.'

'But can I stay? I don't know how long for.'

'Aye.'

'I won't be getting married, you see.'

Stan didn't look the least bit surprised or disappointed. 'Well, no, you wouldn't be here I suppose, if you were. What happened? Did she find out about your Kate?'

'What do you —'

'Oh, Bob had a few whiskies and told me all about it, soon after Alice left us. So you may as well be straight about it, if it's Kate you're after. Have you spoken?'

'She doesn't want to know. I tried on the way up yesterday. She wouldn't even talk. I don't know if I should keep upsetting her.'

'Listen, lad: if she's upset that's all right. It'd be a damn sight harder if she didn't give a monkey's. Get down there, lad. What's the point in flying all this way and tryin' once? Come on, stop getting in my way and give her another go.'

'You've changed your tune.'

'So have you, lad. So have you. I bet you bought a one-way ticket, didn't you? I thought as much. Get on with y', out of my way. Here.' He reached into his overalls and threw me the keys to Joyce's beloved Cortina.

'It's not Wednesday.'

'No, well. Joyce wouldn't be too pleased with the state of the house either, so … we just have to make do.'

It took Kate three hours to appear this time, and it was raining of course, but at least I had the Cortina to wait in. She didn't seem surprised to see me. She didn't look angry either. She just looked resigned. 'You're not going to just give up, are you?' she said. I shook my head. 'Well, it's the tearooms on Mersey Street, then.' She sighed. 'I'll meet you there in an hour.'

Water ran in little streams down the face of the teashop windows as I waited in the corner, and it puddled on the inside sills too, from condensation. Mersey Street looked foggy through all this and I kept expecting everyone to pack up and go home, Play Abandoned due to bad weather, but they all just struggled on in the fog of a typical spring day.

Kate turned up ninety minutes later, perhaps hoping I hadn't waited, and she looked less than terrific, herself. The rain had got to her hair and it made her face bigger, more masculine. There were bags under her eyes too, which I hadn't before. She nodded to me like we were just sharing the table and plonked a cup of tea between us.

'What's the course?' I asked.

'Flower arranging,' she said, deadpan, and drank tea like she needed it.

'I guess you're not short of computers, then.'

'Not really. Two'll do.' She sighed then, tiring of the effort already.

'What work do you do?'

Kate signified great impatience by checking her watch, stirring her tea and breathing deeply all at the same time. 'All right, George: I'm a part-timer at the labour exchange, if you think that's funny, but I can't word process to save my life, never mind broadsheet, and I'm earning bugger all and I'm worth even less elsewhere, so here I am, doing computer classes when I'm old enough to know better, all right? That do? If you're offering a job I can go into finer detail.'

'No, no, that's ...' She was staring at me like she might kick me. 'That's fine.' A silence fell. 'Would you like something with your tea?'

'Yes, I dare say I would, George, but I'll have that at home. Have we done here?'

'Don't be like that, Kate. I just thought we'd ... talk.'

'So you said. So talk. How do you know about Tom?' Kate trained her dark eyes on me, her sudden intensity making my head spin.

'Tom?' I hesitated, wondering on risking the truth, but all I could see was Vic with his hand up her jumper, and it was more than I could confess, having watched that, never mind breaking in. 'Soccer. I've come across him in Whinely. A mate helps out with his team. Bob Gallagher.

Do you know him?' She ignored that. 'I've spoken to Tom there. Just hello, and that.'

Kate still didn't reply, she just stirred her tea, inciting a silence in which the true and awful tension of the two of us sitting there together made itself felt. And it felt more awful, the longer we sat there without speaking.

So I took a deep breath. 'I have to say this, Kate. I know you don't want to hear it and I know it's worthless and pathetic, but … I just have to say I'm sorry. I'm just horribly, horribly sorry that I let you down when I did. I don't know if Alice explained about my mum, but —'

'Oh, Alice explained all right. There's not much Alice couldn't explain.'

'Well, what did she say? I didn't … I mean, I didn't know you were pregnant, Kate. If I'd known —'

'Look, it doesn't matter. I'm not interested. Who cares what Alice says about any of this? It's all done with now. I don't know what you expect, coming bothering me about it now.'

'But I made a mistake, Kate. It's not just that I didn't know about Tom. I made a mistake leaving you.'

Kate's eyes darted over me for a second before widening. 'Oh no, George. No. This is ridiculous. I've got to go.' She stood and grabbed her bag. 'There's no point to this.'

'Then why did you agree to see me, if there's no point? Kate?'

She was looking for something I suspected wasn't in her bag, then at something that probably wasn't in me, either. She said a very final, 'Bye, George,' and threaded her way through the tables and chairs to the entrance. She didn't look back. I stood there for a second, staring at her undrunk tea, then followed in a rush when I thought of Tom. By the time I caught up, she was waiting to cross Guard Street, blocked by the traffic. It was raining hard. She had her yellow brolly and I had bugger all. 'Kate!' I called and she turned and frowned into the wind. 'I want to see him!' I shouted, but she found a gap in the traffic and crossed. 'I want to do the right thing by him,' I said, catching up.

'It's a bit late for that.'

'I'm happy to … to provide support.'

'You can keep your money. Leave me alone. Leave Tom alone. It's too late.'

'I've changed, Kate.'

'I don't care.' She turned to me and stopped outside Boots. 'It's simple, George: leave it alone. Stop lurking in the carpark, for Christ's sake.'

'I just want to meet him,' I said, but she'd moved on by then, and I half hoped she hadn't caught the whining tone. 'Love to your mother!' I yelled, and I think she almost turned at that.

# II

A floodtide was marked in black across Stan's front door, and a hill of black carpet lay in scrolls in the yard. It squelched underfoot when I crossed it, and it smelt worse than ever. Inside, broad expanses of dark stone flags had been revealed in the parlour, the furniture pushed to one side. Stan was wiping it with a dirty mop.

'How did you go?' he demanded the moment he saw me.

'She never wants to see me again.'

'Ah!' said Stan. 'Progress! Joyce never wanted to see me again, just before I had her at Skegness.'

'Feeling better then, are you Stan?'

'What's it to you, y' cheeky bugger?'

'You obviously are, then.'

'There's nowt wrong with me. I don't know what you're on about.'

'Stan, I found you in a state. Have you been drinking again, since I left?'

'Yes, that's right, son. I've been missing you so bad I've turned to drink. I've been yearning for you, cruel-like. Stir the beans.'

I followed the smell into the kitchen and stirred the beans, smiling. Stan came in and sat down wearily at the kitchen table, staring at his hands. The palms were very white, with red welts running across from the mop and the bleach. 'I might be letting the sheep go,' he said quietly.

'Not pulling their weight around the house?'

'They're not well,' he said, ignoring me. 'That's why I've had 'em in. I may have had a drink when I made that particular decision, I grant you, but they're not well and I wouldn't have the foggiest about curing 'em. The thing is, George, I'm no bloody farmer. That's the size of it, and I'm too old to change. I'm a bloody night guard, is what I am.'

I looked at him, head down in his blue guard shirt. 'You've been up here a while now,' I said. 'You seem to know a fair bit to me.'

'Don't be bloody kind, lad. It doesn't suit you. You know why I'm up here on this bloody hill as well as I do — because I'm no bloody use elsewhere. That's why. And to annoy buggers like that Vic Thorne, that'd like to turn the whole bloody hill into one suburb. It were a joy to cross that bugger.'

'When was this?'

'Now old Arthur Rigney, he were what I call a worker. Y' don't have to be born to farmin', but y' have to have a feel for it, and a hunger for educating yourself about it. He knew Latin, did Arthur. A lot of those lads did, in his day, like y' said. Now, they could work, and they kept at it till they got it right.'

'We made a bit of headway, before I went back,' I insisted. 'I can give you a hand now, while I sort things out.'

'We've hardly touched it, son. The weather'll undo half of it, come winter, we've done it so poor, and that's just a couple of the inner yards. There'll be no bloody sheep, anyway, once we're inspected — there'll just be a bloody bonfire. And there's the sweelin' — that should be done by now.'

'What's the sweelin'?'

'I don't even know, lad. Don't you see? I may be old, but I'm far from wise, if you know what I mean. Now ask old Arthur Rigney and you might have more luck.'

'He's alive?'

'Of course he's bloody not.'

I gave him tea and sat by the door, exasperated. 'It's over with, lad,' Stan moaned on. 'Was before I was in long pants. No one's bothered. It's only houses they're after now. The farming failed. It's a mess, all of this.'

'Maybe that's all right,' I said, looking out at the rain. 'Maybe a mess is good. You'd never be here if it was a roaring success. I mean, that's why you're up here, isn't it?'

A depressed silence fell between us and I wondered if there were any point in me staying there, after all. Then Stan mumbled, 'Burnin' the hills.'

'What?'

'Grass and heather and whinberry and what-have-you.'

'What are you on about?'

'Sweelin'. It's years since that happened. It's all going to the dogs now. All sorts growing.'

'So let it grow. That's all right.'

'So you keep saying. Damn hopeless mess, if you ask me.' I wasn't going to ask Stan ever again. Then, just when the hopelessness seemed complete, Stan stood with every sign of renewed vigour. 'Right then,' he said. 'Better get to it.'

'To what?'

'The rest of the carpets, for a start. And the shed roof needs fixing, if you're keeping the sheep out in this.'

'You said it was all hopeless.'

'Oh, for God's sake, lad, you can't let that stop you. Won't fix itself, will it?'

'No.'

'Then get your bloody boots on and stop feeding your face. You've got plump, you have.'

'Plump? I've not got plump.'

'You have. You're fatter than sheep.'


We pulled up the rest of the carpets, and found a beautiful stone floor in every room. After a wipe with the black mop they took on an ebony sheen, and we could see that they were polished smooth long before we came along. Stan found some old rugs in the spare room, we spread them and by lunchtime the next day the house was worth living in again. Better than before, if you left the doors open long enough. While we worked, my resolution to seek out Kate again grew stronger, but I sensed that it was no use waiting in carparks any more. I had to face her front door.

It was mid-afternoon by the time I drove up through Soppstone. Turning into Kate's road, my resolution to drive straight up the lane to her door mysteriously evaporated. I told myself the Cortina might get bogged, and parked on the road by the bus stop.

Likewise, I'd meant to walk straight up the lane, but soon found myself skulking in the shadow of the trees instead. I told myself I needed time to think, but really I was just skulking. The thought of being watched — of Kate slowly identifying me as I lumbered up — was for some reason unbearable.

I leant against the trunk of the last tree and surveyed the blank grey windows of the house. I felt the nostalgic sting of nettles on the tips of my fingers, and looked up to the house, then down the hill, hearing a car engine somewhere. Nothing in sight, but the conviction that Vic Thorne was coming still gripped me. I made my muddy way across to the entrance. The door was very big and very blue and very there, but the air of unreality it brought was overwhelming. I found I was scared and touched the worn brass knocker gently with stinging fingers. It was cold and hard and very real indeed. I banged it twice, harder than I'd meant to.

It was a long wait. I imagined how rare such a knock would be up there. I thought of walking away, but just stood there instead and heard steps, then the lock turn and the dry hinges sing, and I let Kate open the door and see me.

I must have expected her to be shocked, because I was shocked instead by her coolness. She laughed. The kind of laugh that's not much more than an exhalation signalling absurdity, with the head tossed back a bit as if miming shock. Then her eyes narrowed and she said 'Hello' and I said hello back in a croak, which again was like neither of us saying anything at all.

'You should probably just go away,' she said after a while. She was still holding the door, as if she still might slam it.

'I can't.'

'Oh yes you can, George. You've done it before, remember? Just put one step in front of the other. It's that way.' She pointed downhill. I stared at her. 'Look,' she said, 'you don't want to hear what I have to say to you, and I can't say I'm all that curious, so …' She was speaking without bitterness, as if weighing an academic question.

'I can't go away, Kate. Not now.'

Kate raised her eyebrows. 'You're more persistent than you used to be, I'll give you that.'

This was so close to a compliment I could have cried. Facing her at last at her own front door, I realised that I could live with anything except having nothing to do with her. Here was the core, the fulcrum upon which the only thing of value turned in my life. 'I can't just walk away, Kate. I can't. Can't you just let me in for a minute?'

Kate sighed. 'No, George, I can't just let you in for a minute. I don't think I can ever do that. I'm not here on my own, you know.'

'I know, but —'

'How do you know? What do you mean, you know?' Kate, the very picture of suspicion, leant over me now, ready to attack.

'I mean, I know you wouldn't be alone, would you? Wouldn't have to be, I mean. A woman like you.'

None of this was washing with Kate, who had her hard hat on — a hard side I was only now properly remembering from years before. I felt the moment slipping. I would never get through that door. She wasn't even looking at me, she was looking over my head, downhill. Turning, I saw the little figure of Tom down near the trees, struggling up through a long river of mud in his blue school uniform.

Tom saw me a second later and stood still, staring. Even from that distance I could see the shock, instantly swamped by undisguised delight. A great smile washed over his face, and over me too, like sun breaking out over that muddy hill, sweeping up in a great gust of pleasure like I'd never known before.

Tom was running, as best he could in the mud. Kate said, 'You'd better go,' but it lacked conviction. She was watching Tom speed up on the gravel and I sensed her curiosity overpowering her better judgement. I stood where I was, and Tom showed every sign of running straight into me, the little twerp. 'Hello!' I shouted early. 'I'm George.'

Tom skidded to a halt not three feet away. 'I know,' he said.

Kate waved him over and touched his hair. 'From soccer?' she asked, frowning.

'Yeah.' Tom reached up and ran a palm across Kate's face. The frown disappeared, leaving her face blank. 'George seems a very nice man, Mum. Are we having tea? Would you like some tea, George?'

Kate was staring at Tom. I didn't blame her — he sounded like Hayley Mills. 'You don't like tea,' she said.

'Yes I do. Only you don't know. I love it. I love tea. Don't I, George?'

'I don't know.'

'All right, all right,' Kate soothed impatiently. 'Enough. Come on.'

She ushered Tom through the door, but Tom stooped back under her arm and said, 'Come on, George.' Kate looked at me, looked at Tom and disappeared with him inside, shrugging. At least I took it to be shrugging. It may have been a shudder, but I followed anyway.

It felt strange passing into that house the right way, after seeing it all wrong before. The rooms didn't seem so sinister or sad now, just messy. Bloody clean, in fact, after Stan's place, except for a pair of muddy boots in the middle of a white rug in the lounge.

I left my boots beside Tom's in the hall. Kate was putting the kettle on and Tom was running around her being super-helpful, fetching milk and biscuits. 'He does seem nice,' he was saying. 'I like him.'

'Yes, Tom. You might have said that already.' Kate

looked a little flustered. She threw a tea towel over the washing in the sink.

'Would you like a biscuit, George?' Tom held the tin up to me like he was paid to do it. How long had I been away — a few months? I swore he'd grown already. He was taller. Some irretrievable change was creeping up on the boy, even as he stood there. A heavy load was being shifted slowly but surely onto those broadening shoulders, his body pushing him on to carry that burden, long before he could even begin to know it.

'Ease up, mate,' I said quietly, and caught Kate glancing at us, spooning out tea. I took a biscuit.

'Do you play soccer, George?' Tom asked, so loud and sprightly now that Kate positively frowned.

'Used to a bit, yeah.'

'That's funny, you don't look like it. You're too fat.'

'Tom!' Kate said sharply. 'What's got into you?'

But I was laughing and so was Tom, which reassured Kate at the same time it confounded her. 'So are you and my mum friends?' Tom asked, extending the biscuit tin yet again. Kate passed us cups, but she made no move to sit at the table, so we stood there in a triangle in the kitchen, facing each other. 'Are you?' Tom insisted.

'Go and play, Tom,' Kate said, out of patience already. 'Go and kick your ball.'

'Do you want to?' Tom asked me eagerly, abandoning his tea.

'No, of course he doesn't want to. Go on, get out while it's fine.'

I'd already moved to put my cup down, keen to

demonstrate my wonderful winning ways with children, but Kate's hard look said drink your tea and go, and I was still standing there when the scullery door slammed behind him. A little wave of chilly air drifted in. 'He's great,' I said.

'He's mad.'

'Yes, he's mad, granted, but he's great.' A strained smile passed over Kate's face. I could feel her holding herself in, confused like me. 'Funny place for you to end up, this, Kate.'

'It's cheap.'

'But are you happy here?'

The smile vanished. 'You've no right to ask that.'

'I know, I know. But I can't help caring whether you are or not.'

'I could be married for all you know. This is crazy.'

'No, I know you're not. Kate Turner would never marry a bloke who left muddy boots on the rug.'

She didn't smile. 'Look, you'd better go,' she said. I glanced at my undrunk tea. 'He's due back, George. You'd better go.'

At the thought of Vic and his big black car I put the cup down too fast, spilling tea on the table. 'Sorry,' I said, and got up to go.

'When you do go, you go quickly, I'll give you that,' she said.

But by the time I had my boots back on and the front door open, the Zephyr was rocking up the drive. Tom was to my right, kicking the ball against the side of the house. He was studiously ignoring the moving car, even though he stood in its paved parking space.

The car's horn blared — a muted, musical warning from an age of milder manners, which must have frustrated Vic no end — but Tom just kicked the ball again and stayed where he was. Vic gunned the engine with the clutch in, to scare him, and the car glided to a gentle stop just as Tom sprang away. Vic threw the car door open like he'd meant to rip it off. 'What's the idea?' he shouted, then he spotted me coming out and turned to face me. 'What are you sellin'?' he demanded.

He came up towards me, and for a moment I didn't know what to say. Tom started acting the goat behind his back, brandishing the money I'd given him months before, miming crazy glee with the note over his head, trying to make me laugh. Hearing something behind him, Vic turned and lunged with surprising speed, snatching the note from the boy's hand. 'This is fifty quid,' he said, amazed.

Kate was at the door by then with her boots on, watching. Tom reached after the money, but Vic held it behind his back and pushed the boy off easily with his free left arm. 'What's going on?' Kate demanded. 'What is all this?'

'I'd say this is a thief, that's what this is,' said Vic, nodding at Tom. 'I found this on him: fifty quid. Did you give him that? No, I didn't bloody think so. Well, lad: where's it from, if you didn't steal it?'

'It's mine,' Tom said.

'You've nicked it. Yours my arse! I bet it's mine. Are we goin' through pockets now, are we?'

'Liar! Liar! Bloody liar!' shouted Tom.

'Eh!' warned Vic, and he moved suddenly at Tom, but Tom was well out of the way, still shouting 'Liar!'

I'd never seen Kate look so helpless. She just stood there with her hands on her hips, defeated already. 'Where did you get it, Tom?' she said.

Vic was only a couple of steps away from me, peering belligerently at Tom, and nothing upon closer inspection endeared me to him. In his hand was the fifty pound note, looking like it had been folded and unfolded a million times since. He'd kept it in his pocket until he saw me again. The urge to now rip it out of Vic's stumpy red hand and give it back to Tom was overwhelming.

'Where did you get it?' Kate repeated. Her voice was sharp like Vic's now — the same tone I'd feared on the day I failed to say goodbye. 'Come on, tell us. No one's going to hurt you.'

'It were a present,' Tom said and looked hard at me, like he couldn't believe I hadn't told her.

Kate followed Tom's look. 'Bye, George,' she said, but I couldn't take my eyes off Tom. He was expecting me to tell the truth. He needed me to.

'And who the fucking hell is George?' Vic demanded.

'Bye, George.' It was Kate again, and I had no choice but to go. Tom just stared after me, and I had to turn my back and go.

# III

Abattoir Park was, if possible, even wetter and muddier than the last time I'd seen it. Common sense told me there had to be a limit to how much water soil could hold, but Abattoir Park defied it. It was well into spring in principle, but the skies showed no sign, bar the absence of snow. Maybe the days lasted longer, maybe the air didn't bite at your fingers the same way — it was hard to tell, such subtleties were lost in the black and white contrast between the dim, sodden valley of Whinely and the blinding sunlight I'd left behind in Fremantle.

I was there to see Tom, of course. Leaving him the day before had cut twice, concern for his welfare at the hands of Vic vying with more selfish worries about what he thought of me — what he might say about me, after leaving him to it like that. His team-mates were out on the pitch in the rain now, weaving through a line of orange, mud-splattered cones. I thought they were wearing matching socks for once, until I realised that was mud too. Tom wasn't among them and I didn't blame him, but I spotted Bob in the stand, eating an orange on his own.

'G'day,' I said in my best Bazza Mackenzie, and Bob looked shocked at the sight of me.

'You're a long way from home,' he said.

'Don't know about that, Bob. How are you?'

'Bonzer.' We shook hands, Bob with more warmth than the last time I'd seen him. He didn't look bonzer — the sodden hood of his parka had pressed his halo of hair down until he looked like an ill-bred poodle. He wasn't working much, he said. 'It'll be the dole, next. If cancer doesn't get me first.'

'That's a joke, right?' I said and he laughed.

The boys started a game, five a side. Tozer watched from the sideline with grim concentration, saying nothing, expecting nothing. Bob seemed to watch in just the same way. 'Has Tom Turner not turned up?' I asked. 'Still a regular, is he?'

'That's why you're here, I suppose. I've told you before what I think of that. You've no right to interfere.'

'It's not a right, Bob, it's an obligation. I'm obliged to help that boy. He's not treated right, and I won't sleep at night until I do what I can for him, simple as that. Look, I've spoken to his mother. I saw them both yesterday, at home. That's why I'm back, for good. I've packed in with Vanessa, I've quit my job. I think I … I think I might have a chance with Kate, after all.'

'You're dreamin',' he said, but he was looking at me in frank wonder all the same. 'I'll tell you one thing: I never expected to see you here again.'

'Yet here I am.'

'Here you are. You must love the woman, I suppose, to leave a place like Australia for a dump like this.'

'I suppose I must.'

He smiled at that, which was enough to make him look maybe ten years younger. 'Well, he's dead keen, your Tom, I'll give him that. Tozer plays him on the right wing most games now, for a spell at least. He's turned a bit of a corner lately. They don't push him around so much now, he gives it back. They know that now, the big 'uns — they've lost a bit of skin to him — so he's doing all right.'

'Has he scored?'

'Can't shoot to save his life.'

We waited for half an hour, but Tom didn't show, so Bob asked for a lift back to his flat. His van had finally packed up — something to do with the wiring. It was a slow drive, heading into homebound traffic at Smallbridge. Rochdale looked no better than the last time I'd seen it and Bob's block of flats looked worse. There was graffiti on the stairwell that was well out of fashion, and a smell in the air worse than sheep.

His living room was bare but for a mattress by the window, a line of books against one wall and a little plastic stereo. Bob had sold his furniture, not because times were hard, he said, but because hard times had made him see that he didn't need furniture. He'd been reading. 'Nomadic peoples know we need no permanent possessions,' he said. 'We walk this earth as custodians of the infinite.'

Which made sense, so we sat on the floor and polished off our beer. Bob got out what he called his peace pipe, which looked exactly like my Grandad's, so maybe he was nomadic too. The sill of the big lounge window was conveniently low, so we put our backs to the wall, stretched our legs and puffed on the peace pipe staring out. As you do in Rochdale on a wet Wednesday. It all felt perfectly right and natural after the second can of Emu Export. Below us spread such an undifferentiated mass of slate, brick and asphalt that smoking peace pipes on the floor, where you got more sky than land, seemed the only rational response.

'Didn't you like it, then: Australia?' he asked.

'Oh, I suppose Australia's everything you imagine it is, Bob. I wouldn't know: I've never been there, not really. Not like I'm here now, God help me. I felt like I never really landed there.'

Bob looked blank. 'Why's that, then?'

'Maybe it was Mum dying so soon after we arrived. Maybe it was just that, who knows? It just seemed so bloody wrong — to Dad too, I reckon. Like we were stuck with each other. It was like losing the ship that got us there.'

'Marooned.'

'Yeah, shipwrecked. That's it. You know Bob, sometimes I think there might be such a thing as inherited memory. I mean, I don't really believe it,' —

Bob was nodding vigorously with big wide eyes like a puppy — 'but it's like there's a part of me that was always pissed off being in Australia, always hot and blind, always dry. It made me wonder, you know: whether maybe I was the kind that should never leave.'

'Course. Course.'

'This is probably bullshit, Bob. Don't say of course.'

'Course. Course.'

'Anyway, I wondered — couldn't help wondering, the feeling was so strong coming back, you know, even smelling the air at the airport — I couldn't help wondering if a kid like me doesn't make some kind of pact with the world as he finds it, which he can't undo. Like a first love, you know?'

Bob sat quietly, then drained his can. 'I like that about first love,' he said.

'It's never too late, Bob.'

'Tell that to Georgie Best.'

'You know what I'm talking about.'

'I do, George, but I don't really believe it. Never have. It just doesn't seem like that to me. More like you get your chance and you take your shot. Game over, check the score. You don't get to go back and play it again, do you? Or no one would lose.'

'What makes you think the game's over, Bob? I'm sure Lucy's wanting to see you —'

'Don't go on,' Bob said, so miserably it was like he'd shouted. 'Each to their own. It's good to have you back, at any rate. I've been a bit down, thinkin' of you soakin' up the sun. It's good to see you with y' feet wet like the rest of us.'

I rang Kate's next day after four, half-hoping to get Tom first, so I could explain why I hadn't told Kate about the money. Kate answered however, and she almost sounded like she'd wanted me to call. She agreed to meet again at the tearooms after her next lesson. I couldn't resist asking after Tom.

Her tone changed then, all systems closing down. 'Tom's fine,' she said. 'You don't have to worry about Tom.'

I sat at the same table as before, but Kate wasn't late this time and she ordered cake, too. She seemed less impatient, less hostile, and she told me a little about her work, which sounded dull. Then she listened quietly while I explained how I agreed to leave, years before.

'What drives me crazy now, is how I let my parents bully me into it. I can't forgive myself for that. Dad used Mum, I think — he knew I was a soft touch with her. But I was twenty-one for Christ's sake, not twelve.'

'But hang on — Alice said it was your idea, to make a new start.'

'My —' We fell quiet and I watched something clear in Kate's eyes. I said, 'Alice,' and her eyebrows rose knowingly. I didn't need to say it. We talked about friends we'd known in Manchester then, none of whom Kate still saw. It began to feel ordinary talking to her and when I joined her on the pavement afterwards she offered a little ironical smile. This made me bold — Kate made me bold now, and I'd waited a long time for someone to do that — so I touched her elbow and nodded down Mersey Street. 'Come on,' I said.

She shook her arm away and stood her ground, saying, 'Where? Why should I go anywhere with you?'

'Without spontaneity you cannot succeed,' I said, which was pathetic — one of Tom's quotes, popping into my mind.

But strangely enough I saw in Kate's weary face a little life blossom. I recalled a younger, more mobile face that easily switched from sullenness to delight like that. 'That's a curious theory,' she said.

'I'm a curious person.' I took a big theatrical step, then another and she hesitated, then followed and before I knew it I was leading her down to the markets. We found sad little record stalls there, on trestles under plastic canopies, in the shadow of the old viaduct.

'Remember this one?' I said. It was the Inspiral Carpets, of all God's creatures, and it wasn't even their best.

Kate's face lit up immediately. 'Of course,' she said. 'Awful, wasn't it?'

'We'll have that, then,' I said, and tucked it under my arm with exaggerated relish, signifying What Luck. At the front of the milk crate was 'Thriller' and I grabbed that too. 'That's rare, that is,' I said and Kate laughed.

She picked up something by Cindy Lauper, a little bashfully. 'Only a quid each,' the guy behind the stall said by way of encouragement, but he said it sadly and he stayed firmly in his folding chair, out of the wind.

'Worth every penny,' I said, showing Kate a ruddy Max Bygraves. 'This is a gold mine, this is. I'll have the lot.'

'Y' what?' The stallholder got to his feet, as if to stop me buying such crap.

'How much to take the lot? There's no more than — what, thirty? Thirty quid for the box-load, how's that? But I get the box.'

I suggested I give Kate a lift home, since she'd taken the bus, and she accepted casually enough. We put the milk crate on the back seat, probably scratching the upholstery for the first time. I drove straight up the muddy lane for the first time too, to the black house on the rise. When we stopped I let the motor run and we sat there for a moment listening to it hum. 'The thing is,' I confessed, 'Stan doesn't have a record player.'

She actually laughed at that, which made me laugh too, in sheer relief. 'Come and have a listen, then,' she said. 'If you must.'

I was glad to see no Zephyr by the house, and also glad, strangely enough to find Tom out. We had to stand in the hall together, pulling off boots. It felt intimate with just the two of us, like we didn't know each other at all. I asked after Tom, and Kate said he'd be at the park, training. 'We kept him in last week, on account of the thieving. Well, you saw that. I honestly don't know what's got into the boy — he's so rude to Vic. I'm at my wits' end.'

She looked up at me then, shorter than ever with her boots off, and she seemed to regret saying anything. 'I got the impression he didn't think much of Vic,' I said, but she just gave me a dark look and waddled off in her socks to fill the kettle, so I shut up quick.

I set the crate on the rug in the centre of the lounge room and rifled through the contents. Kate came in with tea and knelt down, pulling out records and spreading them over the floor. I sat on the floor with my back against the sofa, watching her. She seemed quite excited about the records, and put the Stone Roses on straightaway. I wondered what the last music she bought was. There was no CD player in sight, just an old stereo.

Her socks were mustard yellow — far and away the brightest thing I'd seen her wear since returning. She turned and caught me looking at them. 'Well, look at yours,' she said, nodding at my purple Mister Perfects. I was thinking of our day in the country, ten years before, and seeing again Kate's bare feet, very white in the sun against the damp grass. I didn't tell her that, but I dared to smile and it was as if she knew. 'I just loved this,' she said, talking about the music, and she leant back against the sofa by my side and closed her eyes. 'I used to listen to this in bed, on the radio. This was just it, then.'

'It was enough, then, eh?' I said. 'You could just dance all the crap away, like there was no tomorrow.' We were both quiet then, both thinking I suppose of all the tomorrows that had come and gone since then. 'Do you know what I thought, when I saw you going into that school?' Kate shook her head, eyes still closed, head back against the seat. 'I thought you were doing art classes. You used to talk about doing art: going to art school and all that.'

'Yes, George, I did.'

'So what happened?'

She opened her eyes, turned to me and raised her eyebrows, flustering me.

'I mean, why the computing?'

Kate took a long deep breath of patience. 'I'd be wasting my breath,' she said. 'I don't believe you have the faintest idea. You think I'll ever be able to support Tom and get him to a decent school on art classes? You've been away too long, George. You've got too soft. Maybe you always were. God, George, I could have a go at you about all the bloody things you've never had to do.'

'I know, Kate.'

'I wish you did. I wish you knew half of it.'

'Give us a break, Kate.'

'You're sitting on my carpet, aren't you?'

'Er, yes, strangely enough, I am. So maybe you don't really think I'm the total shit you make out I am.'

'I like total shits,' she said and laughed.

'I've noticed.'

She took the Stone Roses off and put on U2. 'I hate U2,' I said.

'I know.'

We tried exchanging the glare but we couldn't help smiling. So much lurked there in the silence between us, and suddenly so much of it seemed good. Maybe it was the music, but the memory of a lot of laughter seemed to be percolating through. 'I don't mind them so much any more,' I said.

Kate got to her feet to turn it down. A silence fell. 'Has it been hard, Kate? Seems like it.'

Kate shrugged. 'No point complaining,' she said. 'Short contracts don't help. Odd hours, all that. But you get on.'

'Is that what the course is for: to get on?'

'With a few new skills I can double my pay, and if I get the right position, maybe a longer contract. That's all it is. It's not my dream of dreams or anything. I'm not proud of it, and I'm not ashamed of it either. It's just what I have to do, to pay the rent.'

'What about Vic, does he earn?'

'Oh, Vic's going to make us all rich one day, Vic is.' She waved the subject away with an arm. 'Did you really expect to find me a rich and fabulous artist?'

'Why not?'

'Oh, something to do with talent, maybe.'

'Bullshit, Kate. You draw like an angel. I haven't forgotten — I hope you haven't forgotten. I loved those drawings.'

'Not having the right connections, then. The right surname.'

'Bullshit again. Sorry Kate, but bullshit. I can't believe I'm hearing that from you. The Kate Turner I knew would never say that. She'd try anyway.'

'Well she's gone, George. She disappeared and got replaced with Kate Turner the older, wiser single mother of one, with no qualifications, no credit and friends that don't seem to remember her all that well.'

'You sound almost proud of it.'

'I'm proud of doing a crappy computer course at the Betty Boothroyd, if that's the best offer, yeah. Whatever you think.'

She wasn't particularly angry, saying this — there was the calm determination of low expectations about her, and it bothered me more than anger might. I remembered it surfacing years before, recalled flinching away from it then, from that tone of expected failure, from that narrowing of the eyes and that stubborn chin.

Except life away from Kate, and even away from the difficulties of life here, had only made me appreciate her determination and stubbornness more, knowing so well that I lacked such qualities myself. 'I was thinking of taking art classes myself,' I said. 'At the centre. That's why I was there.'

'You? You don't have an artistic bone in your body. What work do you do now?'

'Law. I worked in law.'

'I rest my case: you're a lawyer.'

'So was Chagall.' That silenced her, and just as silently I apologised to Chagall, who as far as I know never did an honest day's work in his life. 'Give us a bit of credit, Kate. There's such a thing as personal development, you know.' Kate's eyebrows indicated that the jury was still out on that one, but she didn't say a thing. Included in the things she didn't say were shut up, stop talking rubbish and get the hell out of my house. She just drew her knees up to her chest and weighed me up sceptically with bottomless black eyes. The fabric of her slacks was drawn up tight against her thighs, and two luminous calves peeked out above her socks, conspicuous in the dim room like unspeakable memories.

'Odd place to end up, isn't it? For a city girl.'

'Rent's low.'

'There's got to be more to it than that.'

'No, there hasn't. Not if you can't afford a house anywhere else, there hasn't. It suits me well enough,' she admitted. 'There's room up here. Tom can get out a bit and ... do whatever it is Tom does out there.'

'Do you get out walking yourself? With Tom, I mean?'

'No, George. No, I don't. Look: why do I feel like all these questions are criticisms? You don't know the first thing about me and Tom.'

'No, it's just that I like it — the country around here. I never noticed it when we lived in town. I'm thinking I'll stay. I've no reason to leave now, you see. I've broken up with my girlfriend back in Perth, and I've quit my job there.'

'Girlfriend? You're getting too old to have a girlfriend, George.'

'Well, fiancée actually.'

Kate looked like she was seeing the greatest shit that ever lived, which perhaps she was. She started shuffling albums together, and sleeving Billy Idol.

'You haven't asked me why.'

'You're a shit, George Fielden.'

'You haven't asked me why.'

She made to get up, but subsided just as quickly, catching my eye. 'Oh, I think I might know why,' she said and sighed. U2 had done their worst and there was just the wind under the door to listen to, a muted echo of the roar outside making the house sound alive. Kate glanced at me, feeling watched, and she frowned but it was more like she didn't know where it hurt.

She was only an arm's length from me, bowed forward with dark waves over her face and when she looked at me again her eyes seemed to have deepened and darkened again, as if the room had dimmed. 'I was just a stupid kid,' I said, and it came out as a whisper, upsetting us both. 'I just want to make it right now. I still feel as if it's up in the air. Like it wasn't so long ago, you know?'

She nodded a little then, and I didn't know what to say, expecting an argument. I just sat there like an idiot with the soundtrack to Grease in my hands, watching her dark hair bounce gently as if she were crying, but knowing she wasn't. Her presence grew huge in the silence, until I thought I could sense what it felt like on the other side of the invisible wall between us, where we could breathe easy and trust ourselves to smile.

Her lips were pressed anxiously together, as if to kiss a stranger politely, drained of all the irony and fight I knew they could hold. She turned to me and we stared at each other for a second, almost belligerently, as we'd never done before, I swear. We both wanted to kiss — I knew that with a shock down the back of my neck — and we would have too, if Vic hadn't blundered in, shouting, 'This fucking mud!'

# IV

Vic Thorne came through the front door in his favourite leather jacket, black from head to toe, stamping his feet on the mat. When he saw us jumping up like guilty teenagers he stopped stamping. 'What the hell's all this?' he said. His boots trailed dark chocolate across the rug as he came up and I could smell sweat and aftershave.

'We've bought some old records, is all,' Kate said, getting up. 'George here has.'

Vic was watching Kate collect a couple of teacups and straighten her clothes. 'Ah yes, so it turns out you're the famous George, eh?' His hair was no deeper than the shadow on his wide, hard chin. 'And what are you doing on my floor, George?' he said mildly, frowning at me, coming closer.

'You've got mud on the rug,' I said.

Vic stepped back to see it, frowning, and Kate smiled, taking the cups out to the kitchen.

'Fucking mud every-fucking-where,' he said, then looked back at me, close. I stared into the blank grey eyes of Vic Thorne and I couldn't see a damn thing there, unless it was the effort of looking that hard. I recognised the look, from all those obsessive clients happy to bankrupt their families for 'justice': he'd do anything required to win. Anything. He'd start something — prodding a bloke's chest, or just standing too close — and he'd have to do whatever it took to see the thing through. No particular reason, mind, but what else could he do?

'I know who you are, mate,' he whispered. 'She's told me all about it, only I didn't know it was you the other day. I'm amazed you can show your fucking face around here.'

'Vic — the mud,' Kate said, back at the doorway with both hands on patient hips. 'Can you get those boots off, love? I don't need the mud. I can't get it out.'

A broad smile instantly flickered onto Vic's face. 'Nice to meet you at last, at any road, George,' he said, and tiptoed back to the front door with lugubrious delicacy. 'I've told you before, pet,' he called, 'the sooner we're out of this, the better. Out of this fucking mud. I'm sick of this.'

Kate was putting the albums back in the crate, but she didn't act like I should take them and go. 'Vic wants us to move,' she explained instead.

'Not now!' Vic called from the hall.

'Vic's bought a bungalow, down near ... where is it, Vic?'

'We can talk about this later,' Vic said, coming back with a hostile glance at me.

'Is it Shaw?'

'Yes. Look pet, I've told you: you wouldn't have to move unless you wanted.' He laid a heavy possessive arm over Kate's shoulders. 'You can stay in this friggin' mudbath until Doomsday, if you want. I only want what's best for you and the boy, you know that.'

'So what's the point in moving?' I ventured to ask.

Kate and Vic exchanged raised eyebrows, signifying that the Bleeding Obvious had just passed me by. 'A little thing called money, George,' Kate said. 'You probably don't have to worry about it, but if I'm not paying rent, it's a real boon, for me.'

'But you'd like to stay here?' I persisted. 'You'd be more independent, staying?'

Kate exchanged another look with Vic, less complicit this time, as if a serious disagreement lurked under the surface. 'Well, I've a hundred-year lease, so I'm reluctant —'

Vic stepped back, pushing two palms up in protest. 'I've told you, girl: it's up to you. But I reckon once you've thought it out, you'll jump at a decent little bungalow down the hill, out of the bleedin' mud and the weather you get up here.'

'I love it up here,' I said.

'It's a fucking train crash up here, is what it is,' Vic said. 'Tourists might like it, but it's no place to raise a family. We'd be much happier down in Shaw, love.' He put his arm around her again, as if afraid she might run off. His voice had softened now, his tone turned solicitous, and Kate seemed to relax against the bulk of him. 'That's all I want: for us all to be right, y'know? Tom'd be better off too, out of this lot. We don't even know where he is half the time, up here. He needs a good school, if he's to make a success of it.'

'I've seen success,' I said. 'I'd rather be here.'

'Well that's very interestin', George,' Vic said. 'Glad you're havin' a nice holiday. Now, since you are here, George mate, there's a bloody big case needs liftin' from the car. Come and give us a hand, eh?'

Kate was watching, so I had no choice but to follow Vic out. We put our boots on, walked out and Vic opened the back of the Zephyr. I got a hand to the large case inside and said 'I'd hardly call it heavy,' but Vic grabbed my collar and swung me back hard against the wet stone of the house, knocking the air from my lungs.

'Listen,' he said, then clearly wondered what to say. I pushed at his chest with both hands, but he had a thumb in the hollow of my neck, and squeezed effortlessly against my windpipe until I thought it would break. 'Listen,' he repeated, and his face went red. He was struggling to stop himself from really hurting me, and I went loose to help him. He took a deep breath and put his face close to mine, until I stared at his mouth. 'You're not going back in there,' he said. 'You're not saying bye bye, all right? You're not going in there at all, ever. And you're never' — bang went my head against the wall — 'never, never' — again, twice, my head tapped with nicely judged force against the wet, unyielding face of

Kate's home — 'coming back. All right?'

He didn't wait for an answer. He just let me go and carried the case inside, slamming the door behind him.

I was left with a sore head and a good view of the way out. I could just see the Cortina through the trees. It wouldn't have taken two minutes to be out of sight, and Kate wouldn't even have been surprised. But I just took a deep breath and went straight back through the front door instead. I found Vic with Kate in the kitchen, saying, 'Your George had to go. He does nick off, dun't he?'

He saw me taking my boots off then, and the angry flush returned to his face. 'Oi!' He hurried at me. 'I thought you'd gone,' he said, and I recoiled from his hot breath and jutting neck.

'Vic!' Kate called, outraged.

Vic turned back to Kate, and they faced each other. He looked set to apologise, but the front door was slamming again and Tom was kicking off boots in the hall. He didn't look so pleased to see me, this time. He went straight past me into the kitchen and raided the biscuit tin. 'Hello,' he said to the room in general.

At that moment, everyone had something to say which couldn't be said. In Vic's case, it was something he'd like to do as well, and it involved personal injury on my part. Tom surveyed us warily and ate his biscuit fast.

'Well here he is,' Vic said. 'Aren't you going to say hello, George?'

'Vic!' Kate whispered.

'Yeah, shut it Vic,' I suggested.

'Don't you tell me to shut it,' he said. Kate put a hand on his arm and held him there. 'I'm not the one that ran away, mate. I'm not the one in the shit here.'

Tom was watching Vic with narrowed eyes, trying to nut it out. 'Not in front of Tom,' I said, but Vic laughed bitterly.

'Why not? Why shouldn't he know? He's never treated me like a father anyway, doesn't matter what I do. Can't do right, can I? Why shouldn't he know? Let him see what his real fuckin' father's like.'

'Know what?' Tom was saying. 'What are you all on about?'

'Nothing, Tom,' I said. 'Look, I'll go.'

'That'd be right,' Vic said, laughing. 'Off again, are y'?'

'What do y' mean?' Tom persisted.

'Oh, this is ridiculous,' Kate said at last. 'Tom, come here, love.' She knelt down beside Tom.

'No, Kate,' I said. 'Not now.'

'You can't keep it from children. He'll hear it the wrong way.'

'Hear what?' Tom demanded.

'Tom, love,' she said. It was the softest I'd heard her speak since I'd come back, and I didn't want to hear it, suddenly, knowing what she would say. 'I knew George a long time ago. We went out together. He's ... well, he's what you call your natural father, love. We were together before you were born. Do you see?'

But Tom was staring straight at me now and it was clear enough that he understood. He understood that I'd lied to him since the first day we'd met. He understood that I'd deserted him not once, but twice. He understood that he'd chosen the worst person in the world to trust.

'Tom —' I started, but he wouldn't be shut up now.

'Why didn't you tell me before?' he shouted. 'Why didn't you tell me?'

Kate, still crouched beside him, tugged at his arm. 'What?' she asked, but he just pulled away, glaring at me. 'Tell you when?'

'When we were out on the hill,' he said. 'He's been out there for ages.' His little finger stabbed angrily at me. 'Up there, watching us. In the Bradley place. Watching you, Mum. Watching you and Vic. He's always there.'

'Tom —' I began again, but Kate had him crushed to her chest.

'Is this right?' she demanded. 'What have you been up to, George? Tell me this is not right.'

'I was worried about Tom,' I said. 'That's all.'

Shock registered in her eyes then. 'I don't believe it,' she said. 'You've been watching the house? Why? How?'

'From the Bradley place,' Tom said quietly. 'He said he were a soccer coach, and he's not, Mum. He's been in here, an' all.'

I felt a hand close over my shoulder and I swivelled around to face Vic. 'That makes you a stalker,' he said. 'Breakin' and enterin', too: that's a prison sentence, that is.'

'You'd better just go,' Kate said, restraining herself from saying more.

I felt Vic's hard tug at my shoulder, and threw an arm high to shake it off. Vic stepped aside surprisingly fast, and I saw his fist contract tight enough to turn the knuckles white. 'I was worried about Tom,' I repeated. 'That's all. I was worried about what this bastard was doing to him.'

Kate's eyes narrowed further. 'What are you talking about?'

'Ask Tom.' Tom stared at me, his eyes burning with things I hadn't seen there before.

Kate turned his head gently to hers. 'Tom? What's he talking about?' Tom just shrugged — Tom Turner, Champion Shrugger — and looked back at me as if to say Serves You Right. I heard Vic snort derisively behind me at the same instant, very quietly.

'Oh God, George. That's low,' she said. 'I'd forgotten how hopeless you were. Vic's been a better father than you'll ever be.' She looked at me, hesitated, then said 'Go. Just go.'

I let Vic's hand stay on my coat this time. I wanted to say look after Tom, spend more time with him, kick Vic out, don't trust him, but I couldn't say a damn thing. I just had to let myself be led like a dog to the front door and get pushed out. My boots came flying after me.

Vic stood one step above me on the threshold, watching me trying to slot muddy socks into muddy boots. He knelt down to my hopping form and spoke so quietly that it made me slow down. 'If you come back,' he whispered, 'or if I find you lurking around here like a fucking pervert one more time, you know what I'll do?

I'll find you and I'll break your fucking legs. Easy,' he said, straightening up. 'Then you can fucking freeze to death, all right? Toodle-oo now. I don't want to get my feet dirty, kicking your fucking arse.'

There was probably more, but I was walking by then, and all I could hear was the squelching of my boots down the muddy lane, and the wind moaning in the trees by the side of the road. I only looked back once, when I was out of hearing, and Vic was still there on the porch by himself, silently laughing like an idiot child.

# V

Stan brought in a package on Friday morning and lumped it on the cottage table. I was upstairs, staring out the window from the bed, disbelieving the streaks of pale blue sky that seemed to be running in across the valley. The fields were empty — Stan had bitten the bullet and sold the last sheep on the sly, while he could.

'Post!' Stan called, and I came down slowly in my socks, feeling the chill from the door.

'Close that, will you, Stan?'

Stan ignored me, of course, and started roughly tearing open the loaf-sized package. 'Take it easy,' I said, and he just ignored me again, his mouth set in that determined way that made me wish he'd start drinking again. Seconds later, Grandma's beloved gravy boat sat gleaming on the table. Vanessa had cleaned it.

'That were m' mother's, weren't it?' Stan said.

'If you say so. Vanessa's sending a message, I think. Some sort of parting shot.'

'They're stubborn, the women,' Stan said grimly. 'And your Kate's as stubborn as the best of them.'

'She's not my Kate, Stan. Never was. I told you that. I can't see her again, so don't go on. That's why I have to go.'

'Oh, aye. So you've said.' He turned to the door.

'Look, have you thought about Alice's grave? I'm happy to pay.'

'We've no use for it, son. There's no one who'll care for it.'

'But there's nothing to show, once you're gone. You're the last.'

'Gone, indeed. Do you mind?'

'Nothing seems to have worked out, Stan — that's what gets to me. No one's made a go of it. This farm's the same.'

'I can't remember the last time any bugger made money on this land, lad. I shouldn't worry now. It's a bit late. Anyway, we wouldn't be here if it were a goin' concern, would we? You said so y'self. Maybe there's life beyond bloody farmin'. I don't bloody know.'

He left then, looking for work in the empty fields. There was still blue in the western sky, more pale and fragile than anything you'd see in Fremantle. A shallow stream of blue, rather than the ocean you swam in over there. I couldn't go back there now, I knew — not on my own. I wouldn't last a summer. Neither could I stay near Soppstone. I wouldn't be able to shop for fear of meeting

Vic, or worse, Kate. I couldn't step out on the moors without looking out for Tom. If I never met them again, I'd still be seeing them in every dark raincoat in the street, in every kid in a park and every speck on a hill.

I wandered out across the northern field, knowing Stan had gone the other way. The blue scraps ahead inevitably evaporated, and my jeans got wet in the uncut grass. There were small white flowers along the wooded border of the combe, at least, and I'd liked to have known their name. A bright green canopy was spreading over the trees as a concession to the notional spring.

I descended the combe in a long spiral through the trees, getting wetter and muddier as I went, then walked along the busy road for a long time, buffeted by cars, following the concrete curb with no aim in mind.

A final visit to Abattoir Park was required. I had to see Tom one last time, even if it had to be from a distance. Then I'd go. Just go.

I sat with Bob, insisting we take a bench near the top of the timber stand, and I kept the hood of my raincoat up. It was Saturday, so it was a real game and an important one, the last of the season. Whinely were playing Topham, the league leaders, and they needed a point or they faced relegation.

Some of the Whinely boys were peppering the net at their end, trying to warm up without prematurely drenching themselves in mud. The opposition were wisely waiting by the sideline, clean and dry. It was hard to recognise faces from that distance, and I wasn't sure if

Tom was there. To make it harder, there was a blanket of mist sagging over the opposite hillside, and loose threads of grey kept snaking down over the pitch.

Bob was hunkered down inside his tent-sized parka, looking depressed. 'I can't keep up with you,' he said. 'You're no sooner saying you're staying and you're goin' again. You're always on bloody walkabout. Where are you off to now?'

'Does it matter?'

'You don't know, do you? You've no idea, have you?'

I shrugged, Tom-style. I couldn't see him yet. Maybe he was late. 'I used to think maybe it mattered, but you know: Perth, Whinely, Timbuctoo, what's the difference?'

'There's not a bloke in this stand that wouldn't choose Whinely last, out of that little list.'

There was a bloke in front of us with a back three feet wide, and he might well have put Whinely second, but he didn't let on. He just ate his chips. 'I was lucky, in a way, leaving,' I said. 'Losing Kate. Because I got to come back. Do you know what I mean?'

'Yeah — you mean you're mad, and you'd be luckier still if you were hit by a bus.'

'Look, I love all this —' I threw a hand out at the mud and the mist.

'Mad.'

'But if I hadn't left, I'd hate it.'

'Mad.' That wasn't Bob, that was the man with the chips.

'I get to miss it, you see: to miss them. To miss

something I didn't even know I had, or wanted. That's something, isn't it?'

'And don't you look pleased. If you get any happier, you'll top y'self. Cheer up, mate, for Christ's sake. The game hasn't started yet. Eh up, they're closer than you think. Look.' Bob was pointing steeply down to the foot of the stand, and I had to knock his arm down fast because standing by the sideline were Kate and Tom, in matching red raincoats. I huddled back into the hood of my coat, dizzy and cold, feeling the grandstand shift in the wind under me.

'What's she doing here?' I said.

'She came last Saturday, too,' Bob said.

Kate took Tom's coat and he ran out to his team-mates. Kate took the second row up, below us, and became just another hood in the small crowd there. I stared at that hood and wondered if it meant anything, her coming. Had she listened to me after all, warning her about Vic? Tom wouldn't have said anything — that was less likely than ever, with me gone, but maybe Kate had her own doubts, now.

The whistle blew two minutes later and the red shirts of Whinely spread like cherries across the width and breadth of the muddy green pitch, followed by the blue and white of Topham. The rain increased almost immediately and it became hard to track Tom as the grey haze built. There was just this meandering pattern of defiantly bright colours drifting as if wind-blown from one end to the other, around an implicit ball. Little groups surged and converged, then parted, apparently at random, and small high cries of protest or entreaty rose and fell, caught or dispersed by the wind and muffled by the threads of mist creeping in.

'This is ridiculous,' I said, but Bob didn't answer.

Between the rain easing and the mist taking hold, there was a moment of clarity. I saw Tom shoulder charging a blue-shirted defender and dragging the ball out of the mud at his feet, then staggering on across a wide black pool on the right wing. Murmurings rose in the crowd, less than a cheer, more an expression of unease, and the hum of the wind through the seats rose in harmony. The mist pounced and Tom became a blur. A whistle sounded. Bob said 'Never.'

'What? Can you see?'

Bob looked at me as if I must be blind and said, 'Doesn't give up, does he? That should have been a penalty.'

The man with the chips said 'Never' without turning, low like an animal lost in the mist. The ball, presumably, was in midfield again. Kids were charging and scrambling in the mud there, red and blue giving way to grey minute by minute.

'Can't they postpone it?' I said.

'What for? We've never needed to, have we, Bill?'

Bill didn't say and the kids battled on, fighting the weather and the pitch as much as each other, slowing down gradually until they swirled around like dust in the sun. I got one more clear view of Tom with the ball, holding back from the kid in his way, waiting too long it seemed, luring the other in, seductive, patient, more confident than I'd ever seen him before. Then, as he seemed to stop and look back, a quick turn over the ball and he was speeding past, straight at the goal area, hovering over the ball with his feet apart, teasing out space. A delicate feint to the left, and he was lost in the mist to the right.

'Does anyone ever score, Bob?'

Bob shook his head. 'Not funny, mate. You shouldn't take the piss when you're two goals down.'

'I didn't see any goals.'

'Neither did our bloody goalkeeper, but it's two–nil all the same.'

The whistle blew half-time, and the patchy crowd below thumped out the muffled applause of the well-gloved. As Tom crossed the sideline, the noise rose fractionally and I felt my heart skip.

'Hear that?' Bob said. 'For your Tom, that. He's done bloody well, really. We might not lose this, yet.'

I heard them cheer Tom and I'd never heard a sweeter sound. Kate had got up with a drink for Tom, but she was keeping a respectful distance while Tozer tore into the team. Her eyes were on Tom in a way I hadn't seen before. Every one of Tom's days and nights showed in her face as she watched and I knew she'd always be there, that she'd be enough to see him through.

Bob and Bill were conferring grimly by my side. 'We'll have to move down, mate, if we're to see the second half,' Bob said.

'Oh, I've seen enough,' I said and stood to go. 'Is there an exit up the back there?'

'Y'what? Look, mate, there's no point gettin' upset about the girl. I told you it were never goin' to happen. You can hardly be surprised.'

'No, Bob. I don't suppose I am.'

'It's like I say, George: leave it, and get on. There's things you can't fix. It's sad, mate, but what can you do? Play the whistle, eh?' he said and I smiled as best I could.

Half-time was up. The boys were dispersing. I saw Clegg, the big defender, pat Tom affectionately on the back instead of knocking him over. Kate sat down again, pulling her coat tight around her, settling in for the duration.

As Bob and Bill moved down, I turned up towards the back of the stand, tripping on the wet steps as I went.

'What about the second half?' I heard Bob call, but I didn't turn until I reached the exit at the back. By then Bob and Bill had already disappeared. The mist rose towards me, swallowing bowed strangers row by row like a flood. Who were these people, these mothers and fathers anyway? What brought them here? Why did they push these kids so? They seemed alien to me again, as alien as on the bus the first day I returned. I opened the fire escape door, saw the grey void beyond and wiped my stupid eyes. Steadying myself in the wind, I said a silent goodbye to them all.

# VI

Stan left me alone that night and drove off to the Throttled Hen to meet Bob and Roy. He'd caught me packing and I'd told him I'd go the next day. He took the Cortina to the pub, refusing to listen, refusing to believe I was off for good this time. 'Nil desperandum!' he shouted as he drove out the yard. 'There's some bloody Latin for you, lad. Nil bloody desperandum.'

I listened to the Cortina struggle up the road, sat on the table by the window and watched the silver light die some, one last time. Was it my imagination, or was it warmer at last? Had something like sunlight moved the mist towards evening?

I heard soft footsteps on the gravel outside, and felt the skin prickle down my back, as if I had something to fear. I got down, opened the door and watched the frail old ewe that Stan called Alice totter over to his door. 'Come on, love.' I said, and steered her to the shed, out of sight. She'd be burnt if she were seen, and she had to be Stan's best friend, once I was gone.

As I came past his front door, I heard Stan's phone ringing, and realised I'd heard it ringing earlier. I gave it another half a dozen rings, then hurried impatiently in and grabbed it. 'Hello?'

Silence. But somehow I knew who it was, straightaway.

'Tom?' I said tentatively. 'Is that you, Tom?'

Silence. I waited. 'Is that George?'

'Yes, Tom. It's me.'

'Mr Gallagher said you were going.'

'That's right.'

'Are you coming back, then?'

'Probably not, Tom. Not for a while. I'm sorry, Tom. I'm sorry for lying to you.' Silence again. 'I saw you play today, Tom. You were great.'

'Did you see me score?'

'No.'

'Oh.' Another bout of silence, stumping me this time. I expected him to hang up. I gritted my teeth for it, but he said, 'I don't care what he says,' and he sounded defiant.

'What's that? What who says?'

'Vic. I don't care. I'm telling on him, when Mum comes home.'

I heard blood beating in my ears against the receiver, a jolt in my chest. 'Is Vic there now, Tom?'

'He's still watching telly, I think. He's says shut up or I'll be sorry, but I don't care. He's a bastard, and I don't care. That's right, isn't it?'

'Where is he, Tom? He can't hear you?'

'Hang on, I'll see.'

'No, Tom. Just —' He was gone. I heard chairs pushed aside, then nothing. I stood there for what seemed like minutes, then there was a racket in my ear as the phone was picked up again at the other end. 'Tom?' I said. 'Is it all right, Tom? Where is he?'

'Well, fuck me!' thundered Vic. Then, with the phone away from his mouth he shouted, 'Come here, you little fucker! What the fuck do you think you're up to?'

I called 'Vic!' but all I heard was Tom screaming back with desperate, rasping defiance, 'I'm telling! I'm telling!'

Then the phone went down.

I stood there for maybe ten seconds with the phone at my ear, then I rang back, but it was off the hook. I had no car, and no rights, but I had no choice either. If I ran it would be quicker than waiting for a taxi — that was the only calculation I had to make.

The sky was a darkening wound as I started up the slope, the Pike the blunt instrument provoking it. There was no question of running up, it was too steep for that, but the wind pushed me up stone by stone like an old goat all the same, and I got to the whistling black monolith quicker than I ever had before, panting like a dog in its shadow.

As I caught my breath, the moon flashed off the plaque bolted to the base of the Pike, commemorating the fall of Napoleon. I ran across the hill full pelt to take advantage of the light, but the sky lowered again and the silver strip of light to the north was closing up. I slowed to a jog and let the path guide me on, rehearsing in my mind what was happening over there, what would happen when I got here, struggling to recall Kate's timetable and when she'd be back.

In minutes — frantic minutes black with panic, the guilt heavy in my chest like fluid in my lungs — in minutes I was over the next hill and past the rock-strewn stream, my boots and trousers soaked, my hair wet with sweat but hot as if baked by the sun. I was soon heading up the face of the stone outcrop, where the ragged crest of the hill touched the purple sky, knowing that I'd see the lights of Kate's house beyond that, fearing arrival already but determined to help Tom whatever it cost me.

I reached the top terrace of stone and pulled myself up over the edge, exhausted. A pool of rainwater lay captured in its concave surface, wetting my jacket and sleeve. The water was cold, and shivered in the wind, catching light that seemed to have no source. I wiped my face with it, as if I might waken then, and not be so afraid.

When I looked down towards the house I couldn't find it at first. Then, as clouds thinned momentarily overhead, I made out a dim square outline of denser blackness below. Not a single light shone within; it was concentrated darkness I was seeing, not light.

I took aim at this and found my way downhill. As I jumped down onto the hard surface of the lane the clouds thinned enough to see the vague silhouette of someone standing in the yard behind Tom's house.

Never, in all my walks across those hills, had I met a single person after dusk. Even so, until I was within a few yards I didn't think of Vic. The image of him in the hall with his hands on Tom's neck was too vivid. That's where they were: in the hall by the phone, waiting for me. But reaching the ruin I saw ahead the shaven head glow pewter under the sky, and saw teeth come out like a blade as he smiled.

'You're a fucking predictable bastard, George,' he said quietly, and it carried in the wind.

I walked on until only the waist-high dry-stone wall stood between us.

'Where do you think you're going?' he said. 'I told you about your stalking, didn't I?'

'I'm going to check Tom's all right. Then I'm going to help him tell Kate about your fucking treatment of him. That's what I'm going to do. It's up to the police then. You can't stop me.'

But the teeth showed again, and his arms came out from behind his back with the hard, straight outline of a length of steel pipe gripped in one hand. 'Tom won't be telling anyone anything, George. He'll be wettin' his pants worrying about me, just like he is now.' I took a step towards the wall and the pipe swung back low and hung there ready, making me freeze. 'When I said I'd break your legs, George, did you think that was just in a manner of speaking? Did you think that that was just local colour, you fucking tourist?'

'This is pointless, Vic.'

'Right. So go back now, while you can.'

'No, Vic. I have to see Tom.'

'You're not seein' any-fucking-one!' Vic swung the pipe between us over the top off the wall, its soft whistle a warning of weight and speed. But it was too late for warnings, because Tom was inside and I was angry too, and I put a hand on the wall to vault it.

Vic moved, I saw light flash off steel and pulled away quickly as the rock I'd touched shattered, splinters nipping my face. 'Step on my fucking land and you'll get that, all right? Don't think I don't fucking mean it!'

But I was already moving aside and had a hand on the wall again. Vic spoke without moving and there was a desperate tone to his voice, so close to pleading it startled me: 'Just fuck off. I don't want to fuckin' do you, mate. Just fuck off.'

Even so, I never doubted he would. I saw the pipe poised, saw his short deft steps towards where I stood bowed over the wall, frozen. But knowing this, and knowing his strength, I looked to Tom's black home and I took the leap towards it.

My feet never touched the grass: something drove into me and threw me back mid-air, back into a hard cascade of stone that fell deafeningly around my head. The loose wall gave in and swallowed me, and we fell together straight to earth, half in, half out the lane.

'What's the fucking matter with you?' Vic yelled, aggrieved.

I tried to stand, but slipped again, with stone giving way underfoot and tearing at my back and legs. Vic was standing over me, and he held the steel inches from my face now. 'Don't make me angry,' he whispered with insane calm. 'Just shut the fuck up and go, all right? I'll do what I can for the boy, all right? All right?'

But there was a noise behind him and he turned. The scullery light was on and Tom stood in his pyjamas framed by the lit doorway. 'Leave him alone!' he shouted.

I struggled to rise, struggled to speak, but a terrible cloud was over me and I could only stumble on the loose stone towards Vic. 'What's the fucking matter with you?' he shouted at me, but I got to my knees and made to step past him to Tom. A great force whistled into my side then, as if half through me like a blunt axe, then again against my legs, blinding me with the pain until the scullery light died.

'I'm telling!' I could hear Tom wailing. 'I'm telling, I don't care! You can't stop me. I'm telling!'

I could hear steps, and doors banging, then it was quiet. I opened my eyes to pure pain and high clouds, torn edges ragged with moonlight, dim stars further south. Coldness ran under me like a subterranean stream, chilling my spine. The air burned my lungs, coming in hot, but going out cold.

Water was falling, heavy and cold in my clothes. I could feel it clawing at my bones, I could hear it. Luddenden, loud water. Blocks of stone and water, walls and chapels and homes all returning to stone, to blocks waiting amongst the sodden peat to trip you. I thought of Stan and felt he was dying, falling like a stone in the wind from an ill-fitting wall, a dull echo soon lost in the grass and gathered.

I pulled at the wet grass by my side and slid off the stones onto earth. My feet seemed to flap horribly at the end of my legs but I kept clawing at the grass and that turned me until I could see the house. Above the roofline were trees, their branches clothed in leaves now, but still out of reach. There were stones amongst the grass I clawed at, breaking my nails as I dragged myself towards the dark house. The scent of burning flesh was in the air from pyres somewhere.

I heard dogs barking, maybe an owl, then steps — wet muddy steps sucked heavily from the earth one by one. Raising myself on my hands, I watched Vic come towards me: he was picking up the pipe from against the scullery wall as he came. 'You can stay out there, then!' he was shouting into the night. 'But you know what'll happen if you tell her a damn thing!'

Something sharp was biting at my waist. I touched it and my hand came away with the heavy wetness of blood. Vic squatted by me, the pipe over his shoulder. There were tears in his eyes. 'What the fuck have you done?' he kept croaking. 'What the fuck have you done?'

Slowly, not knowing why, I reached out and swept my hand across his face, the way I'd seen Tom do for Kate, to wipe away her anger. The blood on my hand merged with his tears as he flinched back too late, stupefied.

Then he was standing, with the steel pipe raised, not knowing what to do except swing it against my ear, and he was still standing there when white light flashed against the yard wall behind him.

Vic turned slowly to watch it, then walked off in a

daze to the end of the drive. I heard the Zephyr coming on, ploughing through the mud, then Tom's voice over it, calling 'Mum!'

Vic stood still with his legs apart, brilliant white in the headlights, his feet firmly planted in the mud and the pipe still in his hand. He turned his blood-smeared face towards me as the engine died and he sighed, as if he were relieved.

# EXTRA TIME

*Nobody is forced to come to the stadium. Nobody is made to sing.*

Eric Cantona

It took three months, but eventually I got to stand in the sun. I was watching light come and go for weeks, lying on the makeshift bed Stan had set up downstairs in my cottage. For four days the weather came good, but by the time I'd found a shoe and my crutch, and opened the door one-handed and stumbled out into the yard, the clouds had always closed in. On the fifth day I got to stand on the gravel at least, staring up at the waves of grey rolling over a white halo which might have been the sun.

In the second week of September it came each day and I felt at last a lukewarm wash of light over my pale arms. Diluted as it was, it seemed to soak all the easier into my bones like water into limestone. It even looked like it might last — on Wednesday morning blue pools were widening and drifting north from over the Cheshire plains.

With the cast still on my ankle there was no question of climbing hills, but it felt like I could see further than ever. The high grassy slopes on the far side of the valley looked nearer, clearer — I saw buildings I hadn't seen before — and the crests seemed to promise impossible tip-toe glimpses of the North Sea and beyond.

I made an effort with the little garden behind the house that afternoon. Over the last fortnight I'd made a fitful start to building low walls of millstone grit, meaning to raise a bed clear of the mud before the weather turned bad. It was precisely the spot where I'd found Stan months before, trying his best to freeze his own arse off.

My main achievement, stumbling about, was to postpone my full recovery, but I just couldn't leave it alone, knowing the clear weather couldn't last. I'd used mortar and set the base deep, not trusting a dry-stone wall to retain in winter — not one built by me, anyway.

It was all but done, really — I just had to place the top stones well, to make the damn thing presentable to Stan, who never looked at it without wanting to kick it over. He couldn't bear to watch, I knew, as I staggered about with one rock at a time, clattering my crutch against stone.

I'd expected something better by now, myself — flowers, at least, to brighten up the yard — but it had taken too long and now it was too late for half the flowers. I'd finish it anyway — I wasn't going to sit around and watch what I had done go sliding down the hill. Enough had gone that way already: most of the hill's topsoil, the sheep, the chapels, farms and families, the forests before that; the culture of the place, too, along with half the prejudice.

So I knelt down again in soil that was still damp in midsummer and set to mixing more mortar, letting the chill seep into my knees, knowing that it hurt in the right way, at least. Perhaps I'd become more like Stan than I cared to admit. Certainly, I expected less, but did more. I'd match him for perversity one day, if I knelt in the mud long enough.

I made the mistake of really looking at the yard around me, in all its grim glory, and my eyes caught like burrs on the thin column of smoke rising from the high midden in the near corner. I was reminded of the pyres that had littered the countryside all summer, though the smell was far sweeter here. The last trek to Soppstone came to me then, in fragments — the darkness, the heady stench, the blood on my hands.

I weighed the black stone in my palm now, recognising that it fitted nowhere along my wall. I weighed it carefully, thought of Kate looking at me with a sharpness that hurt, and I threw the rock hard against the northern wall, smashing it in two.

Gravel shifted behind me and I wondered what to say to Stan, but turning I saw Tom instead; Tom, in a bright red shirt, standing on the far side of the front yard and staring my way as if caught trespassing. I stared back. It was so unlikely, it felt like a memory. He was taller too, a stranger already, making it unreal. I'd been expecting something else — a summons, a writ, a phone call —

and here was Tom, where he'd never been before. It was quite impossible, and I didn't move or speak, for fear of him vanishing.

He swung a foot instead, spraying gravel against Stan's walls and windows. He wasn't looking at me now, as if he were afraid. He'd been like that the last time I'd seen him and the memory came back sharply, for the hundredth bitter time.

Kate had bowed over me with her mouth open, her eyes unnaturally wide and dark. There'd been repugnance in her face — in Tom's too — as they helped me inside, half-carrying me like a bride over the threshold. She hadn't wanted me in there like that, spreading blood on her floor, but she'd taken me in all the same, into the warmth of her home, stretching me out on the carpet to loosen my clothes, down where comfort made the pain real at last.

Terrible that I'd been like this the last time they saw me. It made me get up abruptly, to shake it off, and the damn crutch caught. I tipped forward hard onto my hands, and they slid in the dirt until my face broke the fall.

So the first thing I heard from Tom was laughter. I got up smiling all the same, because he still had the same high girlish laugh, despite his extra height, and I caught the shyness in his eyes as he came closer. It felt like I still knew him — had always known him, long before I saw him for the first time, muttering in the mist on that bare hill.

I sat down wearily on my own wobbly wall and said,

'Well, hello.' He just leant lightly against the house, a couple of yards off, as if he might go at any moment.

'New shirt,' I said, and he widened his eyes in mock wonder. 'I bet your mum bought that. Bet you don't wear it to training, though.'

'Do so.'

'But everyone hates Man United these days, though, don't they? It's not exactly cool, to be a fan, is it?'

'So? Just 'cause everyone hates 'em, dun't mean you change, does it? You can't, can you?'

'No.'

'My team, in't it?'

'Yes, Tom, you're right. There's no changing it.'

'Right, then.'

I nodded, tired suddenly, wiping the dirt from my palms. Sun landed across the eastern fields, then swooped up the steep hillside to the Pike faster still, where it seemed it should slow. 'How did you get here?' I asked.

'The bus,' he shrugged. 'I'm supposed to be at trainin'. New season's startin'. Tozer'll probably call me mum.'

'How is she?'

He shrugged again — Tom Turner, Champion Shrugger — and nodded at my new wall. 'What y' doin'?'

It was my turn to shrug. I saw him giving the yard a good looking over — the piles of timber and old tools, the sheds with wartime green peeling off. It looked random, like jetsam washed in by a long past tide. 'Beautifying the place,' I said.

'Did Vic do that?' He was pointing now at the dirty plaster cast and he looked impressed for the first time. 'He's not gone to prison or nowt, y' know. Mum's been right soft about it — says he's his own worst enemy and all that. Says he meant well, really.'

'Have you told her everything?'

'No point now. He's gone.' There was a pause, then he said very clearly, as if coaching me, 'She won't be told, see, me mum. You have to be patient.'

I stopped myself smiling, knowing he was right. 'Put in a word for me, have you, Tom?'

He smiled with surprising shyness, then jabbed a finger at my new wall. 'What's it s'posed to be?' he asked.

'A flower bed.'

'Oh.' He looked back, as if to go.

'Look, do us a favour Tom, will you? See that gate there? Go through, cross the field to those trees down there, and you'll find Bob Gallagher. He'll be with an ugly old man called Stan. Tell 'em this: tell 'em they were wrong, and they owe me a tenner. Will you do that?'

Tom leapt at this offer, maybe just to get away from me and my dirty little yard. He was soon through the gate and gone. I retrieved my crutch and got to my feet. Over the wall, I could see Tom's head flying across the field, bouncing high as he leapt the heather and bracken that sheep would have kept down. He ran downhill towards the combe and dipped out of sight.

I set to using the rest of the mortar before it dried,

finding new patience, knowing Tom was about. The stone I'd broken fitted well now, its new face orange beside the dark weathered stones on either side. By the time Tom skidded back through the gate I was almost done.

'Look!' he shouted, waving a banknote in the air. It brought to mind another day, when I'd let him down.

'I'd say keep it, but your mum —'

'All right,' he said, and it was already in his pocket. He climbed the field wall and watched as I fumbled about on one leg. 'Stan had a message,' he said. '"Tell him to go to buggery", he said.'

'Thanks,' I said,but Tom was already jumping off the wall into the front yard. 'I'm off,' he said. 'I'll tell Mum I caught the wrong bus.'

'No, Tom. Tell her where you've been. All right?'

He shrugged and kept walking, but I knew he would. On the far side of the yard he turned to look. 'Bye!' I called.

'Ta-ra!' he yelled, and then he was gone.

I found a spot for the last stone, mortared it in place, then hobbled over and leant on the north wall. Bob and Stan were coming back for tea, arguing, of course. Above them, light cloud was caught in a fast gale too high to feel. The sunshine had grown thin and fragile.

Coming through the gate, Stan followed my gaze and nodded. 'We'd best make the most of it,' he said.

# ACKNOWLEDGEMENTS

I'd like to acknowledge the contributions of all at Fremantle Arts Centre Press, and in particular the unparalleled navigational skills of Wendy Jenkins, without whose editorial work this story would never have got home.

My heartfelt thanks go out to Alison and Sylvia Kershaw, to Mark Dennison, Robert Castiglione, Bruce Russell and Shirly Jackson, and to family, friends and Black Skivvies everywhere.

The Moorhouse family of Fielden House also have my undying gratitude for their hospitality.

Eric Cantona's musings (quoted on pages 7, 47, 60, 78, 99, 127, 133, 178, 214 and 249) are collected in *la philosophie de Cantona: A bilingual celebration of Art and Beauty*, edited by Michael Robinson, Ringpull Press, 1995.

I am also indebted to *Millstone Grit* by Glyn Hughes, Victor Gollancz, 1976.